THE COWBOY'S BABYGIRL

A DARK COWBOY ROMANCE

LEE SAVINO

TRISTAN RIVERS

THE COWBOY'S BABYGIRL

Fate brought the pretty little runaway with defiant green eyes and that sassy mouth to my doorstep.

Carrie Smith needs more than shelter.

She needs protection.

Discipline.

A firm hand.

She came to the right ranch.

I never thought I'd have a wild girl of my own to tame.
I'm just the man to tip her across a hay bale and show her who's in charge.

But there's more to this girl than meets the eye.
I may give her the discipline she craves, but she'll satisfy my darkest desires.

She'll be my one, my only... *my babygirl.*

EXCLUSIVE FREEBIE

Sign up to Lee Savino & Tristan Rivers newsletter and receive a special short freebie: *Steele Breeds His Babygirl*

Go here to download: https://geni.us/Steeleandbabygirl

CHAPTER 1

Steele

$\mathcal{I}$ found her curled up on my front porch when I got back from seeing to the cows. With her skinny arms wrapped around a backpack, and stringy blonde hair hiding her face, she looked more like a bundle of rags than a girl.

I dismounted from my gray mare, tied her to a fence post, and clumped up the steps. I was in no mood to deal with uninvited guests. We'd lost a calf during the night, despite my best efforts. It was one of a hundred that had been born this summer, but every last one hurt. I hadn't slept in over twenty four hours, and I was filthy.

My boots thumped on the wooden decking and I stopped right in front of the girl, but she didn't stir.

I cleared my throat loudly. "Can I help you?"

She lifted her head slowly, like a cat, indignant at being disturbed. Then she pushed her hair back with her forearm, revealing a pair of curious green eyes and a snub nose flecked with freckles. When she met my unimpressed gaze, alarm flashed across her face. She uncoiled herself and scrambled to her feet.

Standing, she was no higher than my armpit, with a wan, pale face. I would have written her off as a buckle bunny, looking for a good time with a cowboy, but they usually hung around bars. It was midmorning, and her tight pink T-shirt and faded jeans hadn't seen a washing machine for a long time. A runaway, maybe one of those foreign travelers who drifted through, looking for work in exchange for bed and board.

Looking down at her, I felt a flicker of interest. With those tired smudges under her eyes, she wasn't pretty, but something about her waifish air stirred my protective instinct.

I crossed my arms over my chest to hide any sign of soft-ness. I needed another stray to take care of like I needed a hole in my head.

"Hope you're about to tell me why you're trespassing on my property," I growled.

She blinked at me dazedly. "Heard you're hiring." Her voice was slow with sleep, with a drawling American accent.

I frowned. "No, I'm not hiring anymore."

"But, I saw your ad—"

"The ad's old. It's been a full season. I've gotten all the help I needed. Now, if you'll excuse me…" I stepped past her and opened the front door, hoping she'd get the hint and move on. I didn't have time to deal with a cute young thing who thought it'd be fun to work with horses. My eyes were gritty, my body aching, and I sorely needed to wash up after dealing with the stillbirth.

Her lower lip jutted out in a pout. It would have been

adorable if I was in the mood to play. "I wrote you a whole application, and you never even replied!"

"I stopped checking the replies when I was full up," I said over my shoulder. "No one looks for work here this late in the season."

"Please... just take a look."

There was a thread of desperation in her voice. I stopped, sighed, and reached into my back pocket for my phone. I hate the things, but unfortunately they're necessary if you want to run a business these days.

While the girl stood, arms folded, those striking eyes of hers watching me expectantly, I scrolled to my email app and opened it. Full of junk as usual. "When did you send the message?"

"'Bout a week ago."

"I see a message from fluffykitten666." I raised an eyebrow at her. "That you?"

She nodded defiantly.

Exhaustion was making me ruder than usual. "That's not how you approach a business, seeking employment."

I clicked on the message and it opened. I groaned inwardly. It was a piece of childish nonsense. Badly spelled, with no notion of punctuation.

I held up my phone. "This isn't how you write a job application, either." Hopefully, if I was cruel enough, she'd go.

"Fuck you," she hissed, as mad and spitting as a feral cat.

"Language," I barked.

She dropped her head, glaring at the deck. "It's not like I'm looking to be a secretary, mister." Her snide tone was worse than her cussin'.

Sheesh. I gritted my teeth, palms tingling. *I should take her over my knee.* I ignored the stirring feelings below my belt buckle. One of us needed to act professional.

I cleared my throat. "That doesn't matter one shred.

When you're trying to get hired by a professional enterprise, you can't go acting like a kid in grade school." I couldn't abide poor grammar, especially not in business dealings. My dad drilled that into me at a young age.

I shoved my phone back in my pocket. "Like I said, I'm not looking for staff, and you're not somebody I would hire anyway."

She took a step closer, small fists planted on her hips. For a little thing, she sure wasn't afraid of throwing out challenges. "And why is that?"

I pinched the bridge of my nose. Now I had a headache. "Well, aside from your evident lack of maturity, I need strong workers who know horses real well."

"I'm stronger than I look," she insisted, tilting her chin toward me.

I gave a final, dismissive shake of my head—which made it throb worse—and grasped the door handle.

"Hey." She took a step forward, her voice softening. "I'm sorry if I came across a little riled up. Please, mister, just give me a chance. It took me a long time to get here. I-I really need food and a place to sleep."

I glanced around the yard. There was no vehicle in sight. "How did you get here?"

"Walked. From the station."

From the train station? That had to be a good two hours.

"It was a long way," she said, as if reading my mind.

I looked her up and down again. She swayed a little where she stood on the deck. She needed washing up and a good meal. If she was much more than hundred pounds, I'd eat my hat. One good breeze would blow her away. My resolve was melting. "I don't think you're old enough to work here, anyway."

"I'm nineteen," she insisted. "Almost twenty."

A baby. No wonder she didn't know how to act. But the

4

weariness in her eyes and the light grooves around her mouth made her seem older. Worn out. As if she was holding herself together with desperation and spite.

Maybe I could take pity on her. "Show me some ID."

She hesitated, then dove into a pocket on her backpack, pulled out a frayed canvas wallet, and withdrew a driving license. I reached out to take it, but she held on.

"Here is me. Here's my age." She jabbed at the photo and her date of birth, her thumb obscuring most of the other information. Carrie Smith. Born nineteen-and-a-half years ago. It was a Texas driver's license. I supposed that explained her slow, twangy pronunciation. It looked genuine, not that I was any kind of expert on US IDs.

"Okay. You're nineteen. What are you doing here, up in British Columbia?"

"Seeing the world, like anybody else." She shrugged, but the carefree gesture was ruined by the tension in her body.

We didn't get a lot of Americans looking for work on the ranch. We mostly hired foreigners: Europeans, some Australians, even some South Americans, from time to time. We didn't pay them—we weren't allowed to. It was a work-in-exchange-for-board arrangement.

It was on the tip of my tongue to call her out on her lie, but I bit it back.

"Okay," I said non-committally. "And you know horses?" I didn't know why I was asking her, aside from the fact that she looked like she was close to the end of her rope.

"Sure am. Grew up riding them."

"Let's see what you can do."

I led her over to my mare, Silver, who watched us approach with curiosity. She was a spirited eight-year-old, a little frisky sometimes, but nothing an experienced horse-woman wouldn't be able to handle.

I watched Carrie dubiously as she patted the horse on the

neck. She seemed relaxed and at ease around a horse—a good sign. But then she stepped one foot into the stirrup, grabbed the saddle… and struggled.

She was so tiny, she didn't have the leverage to jump up into the saddle. Instead, she hopped on one foot, helplessly.

"Come on." I grabbed her by the waist and hoisted her. But as I did, my hands slipped past the waistband of her jeans and onto her bare skin. She turned her head, startled. When our eyes met, my breath caught in my throat. She might be a street urchin, but she had the curves of a woman. Her skin was velvety soft, and her behind filled out her jeans like two ripe peaches.

I set my jaw. I shouldn't be thinking about her that way. This was a job interview, and she was desperate. Besides, she was way too young for me. Young enough to be my daughter, if I'd been a teen dad.

I needed to start treating her like the ranch hand she wanted to be. I steeled myself and gave her a hard shove, propelling her over the horse's back.

She leaned forward and fidgeted, fighting to get her foot in the other stirrup.

I went around and adjusted the stirrups, pulling them up several notches until they fit.

"Thank you," she murmured.

I didn't answer, but made my remaining movements brisk. Caring for her, strapping her in—it was bringing up memories. Unwanted ones.

I tilted my hat back. "Sure you know what you're doing?"

"Uh-huh," she said, but there was a flicker of nervousness in her eyes. I paused, seriously considering putting a halt to all this.

But her chin jutted out. "I'm ready now," she said, regal as a queen.

I shook my head but took the reins and led Silver into the large corral that ran alongside the house.

"You comfortable with trotting? Loping?"

"Yup. Second nature," she muttered.

"Silver is a reactive horse," I told her. "She has a soft mouth." I frowned at Carrie's sneakers. Not at all appropriate for riding horses. "Go easy with your heels."

"Yup." Carrie was now staring straight ahead, as if psyching herself up for the task.

"One round of trot, then you lope for one round. Think you can handle that?"

"Sure can." *Lying through her teeth.* My palm twitched, out of habit.

"Off you go." I gave Silver a slap on her hindquarters and she set off at her usual lively pace.

Carrie lurched forward and grabbed at the front of the saddle.

I worked my jaw back and forth. *A horsewoman, my ass.*

Silver began to trot of her own accord. She knew the corral well. I'd broken her myself, as I had most of my horses, and we'd spent many hours here, with me putting her through her paces until she trusted me enough to submit willingly to my instruction.

But Silver had a bouncy gait and Carrie was not handling it well. She was hunched over like a sack of potatoes, clinging to the saddle with both hands. When she turned the third corner and headed back toward me, her face was frozen, her eyes wide.

"Wanna stop?" I called.

"Nope!" came her strangled reply.

The girl had guts, I'd give her that. *She'll be all right.* I'd remind myself until I believed it. She'd come onto my property and sassed me. When I was done, she'd run home with her tail between her legs.

I clenched my fists at my sides, holding myself back from racing to her. Everything in me wanted to forget this sham of a job interview, lift her out of the saddle, take her inside… Give her a bath and let her sleep a while. Cook for her, and see if good food and rest would return the color to her cheeks…

No. That was the old Steele talking. The Steele who was too soft. The Steele who ended up with a dagger in his heart.

Never again.

Carrie's little body was loosening up. She still hadn't gotten the rhythm of Silver's gait, but at least she didn't look like a mannequin tied to the saddle.

"That's it," I said, and she brightened at the praise. Her cheeks flushed and her eyes sparkled. It was like a light bulb coming on, illuminating her lovely face. "Now, keep hold of the saddle and give her a little kick."

Carrie kicked Silver at least twice as hard as necessary.

Right away, Silver bounded into her fast canter. It was her natural gait, and she would run and run until someone told her to stop.

"Woah!" I bellowed and sprinted across the corral.

Silver slowed, but Carrie lost her stirrups, then her grip on the reins. In a panic, Carrie grabbed Silver's mane. Time slowed, and every second became a year as Carrie pitched forward and lay flat along the horse's neck, clinging on helplessly. My heart slammed against my ribs.

The horse pulled up just in time for Carrie to slide right around her neck and fall into my arms.

She was a light armful. Too skinny by far. But she felt right in my grasp.

Then I got a look at her angry little face. Her eyes flashed with enough fire to set my hat ablaze.

"Put me down," she ordered, as if she called the shots here. She hadn't learned her lesson at all.

I forced my breath to calm, and set her on the ground gently, just to make a point. Silver stood quietly, her intelligent eyes flashing with horse mischief.

Carrie immediately headed back to the horse's side. I clamped my hand on the back of her neck to stop her.

"And just what do you think you're doing?" My voice was guttural, my breath still ragged. She could've broken her fool neck.

"Going to ride," she snapped back. "I was doing just fine until you interrupted." Another lie. It set my teeth on edge.

"Let me go." She rolled her shoulders, trying to dislodge my grip. I resisted the urge to shake her like a cat.

I forced her to face me. "You lied to me. That wasn't riding. You could've been hurt."

She glared back at me but didn't argue. For once. After a few seconds, she dropped her eyes, and I made myself release her.

Her clothes now had an additional coating of red-brown dirt. She made a half-hearted attempt to dust herself down. Then she rubbed an arm over her tired face, smudging it. "Yeah, well, it's been a while," she mumbled.

"I won't have the safety of my horses compromised by a foolish child. You lied to me about your experience," I said. "I won't have a liar on my ranch. I can't abide them."

She had the grace to look chastened.

I crossed my arms over my chest, my earlier exhaustion chased away by a new spurt of adrenaline. "Do you have any experience around horses? Tell me the truth."

"I've been riding a few times," she said in a small voice. "Had a few lessons when I was a kid."

"And you thought that'd be sufficient to cheat your way into a job?" I clenched and unclenched my fists. If she was my submissive, I'd already have her bent over a hay bale with her jeans down. My palms prickled, and I wished I could punish that pert round bottom of hers. "Why did you even want a job here when you don't know how to ride?"

"Because I needed it, okay?" she hissed. She was all mad again. A pocked-sized spitfire. A feisty tomboy with a pretty face and curves in all the right places. "Isn't there something else I can do in this place?"

"It's a horse ranch. I hire riders. Not little girls who wouldn't know the truth if it hit them in the face."

She was getting right under my skin. I was done. I'd been up all night. I took Silver's reins and began to lead her out of the corral. "Job interview's over." I made my voice as steely as I could. "Like I told you, I'm not looking for staff."

"Please, mister," she called after me. "I'll do any work you ask." Her voice cracked. "Anything at all. I just need a place to stay right now."

I wheeled on her. The reddish dirt on her face only made her look younger. Her lonely trek out here, her unwashed clothes—she had nowhere else to go. That much was obvious.

But I ran a business, not a charity. I wouldn't take on a freeloader again, no matter how pretty her face. No matter how my body responded to her.

But the desperation in her eyes gave me pause. She wasn't trying to seduce me. And she'd sent in her resume. She wasn't looking for a handout, she was trying to earn her way. Maybe I could help her for a little while.

Looks like I still have a few soft places left in my heart. A miracle. After Victoria, I didn't think I had a heart left at all.

"Fine," I said. "You even like horses?"

She nodded. "I've always liked them. I like all animals. And when I saw your advert, I got a real good feeling about it, and I figured… maybe I'd be happier being around animals than people."

The words came out in a rush, and there was something

so raw, so true, about them that my chest ached for her. Something had happened to her that had scared her badly. Had made her distrust other humans. I wanted to ask her what it was, but now wasn't the time.

Instead, I looked her up and down and sighed.

"Okay, how about this. You can stay—just for a couple of days. Help me out with some odd jobs. But any more sass, and you're gone. I'll drive you to the station and put you on the next train myself."

A mixture of emotions—relief, disappointment—passed across her grubby little face. "Okay," she said at last. "Thank you."

Outside the corral, I untacked Silver and let her loose in the open fields.

"Now, shake my hand," I told Carrie. Her hand was tiny in mine, but her grip was surprisingly firm, and she met my gaze with determination.

"You can call me Steele," I said.

"Steele," she repeated and, heaven help me but I liked the sound of my name on her lips.

I handed Silver's bridle to her. "Help me carry this."

Maybe all she needed was a little discipline. If so, she'd come to the right place.

CHAPTER 2

Carrie

When we were done putting the horse stuff away, I followed Steele's tall, broad figure up the porch steps, hugging myself. Trying to stop the shaking that had taken hold of me.

It was dumb of me to have lied about my experience—I knew that.

But it was all I had. And I was desperate.

I'd been running panicked, scared, for weeks, until I was down to my last handful of dollars. I'd hitched rides; sneaked on a train; slept in bus stations, a restroom, around the back of a gas station, and even, one awful night, in a ditch.

Then I'd seen Steele's ad, and gotten a stupid notion that I could hide out on the ranch and work with the animals. I pictured myself taking care of them—safe among their simple natures, sheltered from the world. They didn't trick you like humans did. They didn't tell you one thing, then do another.

I hadn't figured on their owner being so damn intimidating, though. That gruff, unfriendly way of his. His straight-backed, broad-shouldered bulk. The way he'd picked me up off the dirt like I weighed nothing. That uncompromising set to his jaw.

But his eyes were shrewd—like he could see right into me; see all the dirt and mess and sadness.

And for some reason I couldn't understand, he was giving me a chance—even though I'd made a giant fool of myself.

That meant he was kind, at least.

"Pick up your backpack," he ordered.

He was also someone who was used to being obeyed.

I snatched it up from where I'd left it, full of every single thing I owned in the world.

"I'll show you around," he said as I followed him inside the ranch house.

There was a small, neat kitchen. The countertop was polished to a shine. No crockery in the sink or on the drainer; a dish towel folded neatly over the oven door rail. Off to the side was a wooden dining table and four chairs, and beyond that, a comfy looking sitting room. Down a corridor was a modern bathroom, all bright and sparkling.

"Are you married?" I blurted out.

He paused in the tour. "No, why do you ask?"

I shrugged. "No reason. Seems real clean in here."

Some emotion shadowed his face, but he only said, "Cleanliness is a virtue."

In the mirror above the basin, I caught a glimpse of our reflections. Me looking like a street urchin; him towering more than a foot above me, his plaid cowboy shirt straining across his huge shoulders. He was a lot older than me, but drop-dead sexy. All muscle; all masculine—from his broad jaw and sharp cheekbones, to his firm, pale lips. His skin was tanned and weathered, offsetting the inky blue of his narrow eyes. I couldn't see what color his hair was, as it was hidden beneath his black cowboy hat, but his eyebrows were dark brown and thick. He smelled of fresh air and horse leather.

He turned suddenly, and his arm brushed mine. I wobbled, weak from lack of food and sleep, and for the second time that day, he caught me. His arms were ridiculously big and hard with muscle, his body strong and rugged as a rock hewn from the nearby mountains. I was safe, swallowed up in his arms. His warmth seeped into me, and the chill I'd carried in my bones all these miles started to thaw.

"Careful." His voice was a rumble in my ear.

I gave a shaky nod and pushed off his firm chest to stand on my own two feet.

"This is your house? It isn't much."

I instantly regretted mouthing off. His house was a lot nicer than any home I'd been in. "I-I mean, with all the land around, I expected a bigger place."

He gazed down at me, a single dark brow arched. "Careful," he repeated, and my cheeks flushed. I ducked my head, all the sass draining from my body. I didn't know why I mouthed off other than because I was tired. It wasn't even nine am, and it had already been a long day.

Steele motioned down the hall, which ended in a bedroom. The door was cracked and I took a peek. It looked cozier than I'd expected, with rustic looking pine furniture, and a blue comforter spread neatly over the king-size bed.

"That's it. Tour complete," Steele said.

But where am I supposed to sleep? He might be the sexiest older guy I'd ever seen, but that didn't mean I was ready to share a bed with him. Panic prickled in my gut.

"I've got a bed for you out back, where the travelers stay," he continued.

Phew.

He clapped his hands together. "Now, let's get you washed up." He gestured to my backpack. "Got anything clean in there?"

I shook my head dumbly. The clothes in there were even dirtier than the set I was wearing.

"Give me all your laundry," he told me, "and when you go in the bathroom, put your dirty clothes outside, too. I'll put them in the washing machine for you."

I opened my backpack and handed him two T-shirts and a pair of shorts, then hesitated.

"Anything else?" he said.

My cheeks warmed as I pulled out two pairs of panties and a bra, and stuffed them in the bundle with the rest.

"There's a fresh towel in the airing cupboard," he told me, "and you'll find soap and shampoo in the shower."

I went into the bathroom, pulled off my filthy clothes, and dropped them on the floor. I felt dazed by all the instructions. But a small part of me liked being ordered about like this. It was nice not having to make decisions for myself for once.

As I turned to step into the shower, there was a knock on the door.

"Carrie? I told you to pass me your dirty clothes." There was a harder edge to Steele's voice now. Hurriedly, I picked up my T-shirt, jeans, panties and bra, bundled them up, and opened the door a crack.

For a moment, I wondered if he was going to push the door wide open. See me naked. A part of me wanted him to. But he stayed outside, only his big, callused hand coming into view. I shoved the things at him with a whispered, "Thank you," and shut the door again.

The shower was *amazing.* Rainforest style, and so hot and steamy. It was literally the most luxurious experience I'd had in my entire life. I scrubbed myself from head to toe, washing a week's travelling grime off of me.

When I was done, I wrapped myself in a towel. It was rough—a guy's towel—but it smelled fresh.

I felt transformed. Like I was leaving the fear and ugliness of my past life behind. I didn't know what lay in my future. I was still in trouble. And Steele said I could only stay a couple of days. But at least he'd given me this—this moment of kindness.

I eased open the bathroom door, embarrassed at the thought of emerging in just a towel. But something dropped to the floor on the other side. It was a red plaid shirt, which must've been hanging on the other side of the handle. I retreated back into the bathroom with it. It was obviously Steele's shirt—massive, and softened from being worn often. I pressed it to my face and inhaled. It smelled of fresh laundry, but I wished it smelled of him instead: horses and hay and manly sweat. I put it on and buttoned it up. It was comically big on me, falling down to my knees. I rolled the cuffs until they no longer hung over my hands.

My hair was all tangled, as usual. I found a tortoiseshell comb in the bathroom cabinet and combed it straight with a neat parting off to the side. My hair was wispy, and never grew much past my shoulders.

I hung the towel on a hook and hesitated at the bathroom door, very aware that I was naked under the shirt. There was nothing touching me between my legs. Nothing protecting me.

Since Steele had taken my underwear, he would know that, too.

The thought made me feel hot and squirmy.

"Everything okay?" came Steele's deep voice.

Dammit. He'd probably heard me fiddling with the bathroom door.

"Coming," I called, and took a deep breath.

When I emerged into the kitchen, Steele was standing at the stove, frying something in a skillet. He was no longer wearing his cowboy hat, and his hair was tawny colored: short on the sides, but longer on top, and a little mussed. It was sexy—less ordered than the rest of him. His eyes roamed over me from head to toe, and I felt even more naked. My cheeks warmed.

Finally, he cleared his throat. "You clean up nice."

I didn't know what to say, so said nothing. I'd braided my wet hair, thinking it was an appropriate hairstyle for a cowgirl. I fussed self-consciously with the ragged end of the braid.

He nodded toward the dining table. "Take a seat over there. It'll be ready in a minute."

Holding the shirt tight around my body, I shuffled across the room, the wooden floorboards smooth beneath my bare feet. I dragged out a chair and sat down.

Steele clicked his tongue. "Lift, don't scrape."

"What?"

"The chair."

"Oh. Sorry."

He nodded and turned back to the stove.

Wow. Dude sure has a thing for rules.

The silverware was set up neatly on the table, with a folded napkin and water glass.

I bunched the spare fabric of the shirt between my thighs, and watched him discreetly as he worked. Despite his bulk, he moved fluidly, every action spare and precise. And whatever he was cooking smelled wonderful.

A few minutes later, he put down a plate of eggs, bacon and pancakes. My stomach growled like a hungry beast, the sound surprising me. The loud gurgle seemed too big to come from my small body.

Steele seemed to think so too. He gave a snort of a laugh, and amusement eased the sternness from his features. "Been a long time since you ate?" he asked, standing at my side.

I nodded. "Yeah, I think so." I'd mostly lived on gas station snacks for the past two weeks.

The silverware was set up neatly at the table. I picked up my fork in my right hand and started to eat.

"Now, Carrie..." came Steele's deep voice. "You eat at my table, you hold your fork in your left, your knife with your right."

I blinked at him. All my life, I'd been eating one-handed. I hardly ever ate anything that needed cutting up, in fact. "You sure have a lotta rules."

He raised a brow. "That's right. If you stick around, you'll learn them all."

Ugh. "Were you in the military?" I demanded.

He nodded, the grooves along his mouth turning serious. "Yup. Four years in the army. My father was, too. He brought me and my brother Max up with an appreciation for discipline." He loomed over me, taking my napkin, and smoothing it onto my lap. "I can tell you haven't had a lot of order in your life, Carrie. But you'll find that it fills you with a sense of purpose, and gives you a lot more freedom."

Frowning, I transferred my fork into my left hand, just like he'd told me, and dug into my pancakes, struggling to comprehend what discipline and freedom had to do with each other.

The food gave me energy, and my body started to wake up. I started to eat fast, but that didn't impress Steele either. He gave me a ton of instructions: how to position my fingers on my fork, not to talk with my mouth full.

"Yes, sir." I pretended to salute him with my fork, and he frowned at me.

"You'll thank me for this one day," he said.

I opened my mouth to retort that I wouldn't, then realized how childish that sounded.

The look in his eye startled me. It was full of kindness. No one had looked at me like that before. "It doesn't matter whether you're on a ranch, or eating with the queen of England," he said. "Good table manners will see you right, anywhere."

I shrugged. *Guess he has a point.* My whole life, we were lucky if we even ate off a plate. Usually, we were sitting on the couch, with the TV blaring and the room stinking of smoke.

"There's just so many rules to remember," I mumbled.

"That's right. Especially out here on the ranch. Rules are important, they keep you safe." He gave me a look that made my mouth go dry. "If you want to stay around, you'll follow my rules. And if you break them, you'll accept the consequences. Understand?"

I ducked my head, but that wasn't enough for Steele.

"Answer me, Carrie. You want to stay here, you abide by my rules. Disobedience has consequences."

"Got it." My nonchalant answer didn't seem to appease him, but after a moment, he grunted and left it alone.

I kept stealing glances at Steele while we were eating. The knife and fork looked tiny in his big hands, but he handled them like a surgeon or something.

I remembered how one of those hands had touched my bare skin this morning. It had been an accident, I knew that. But a silly part of me wished it hadn't been.

The moment we were done eating, I jumped up and grabbed his empty plate. Surprise flashed in his eyes, then approval.

I wanted to please him, I realized. To win his respect. The feeling kindled inside me like a flame.

Steele got to his feet, too, and showed me where everything belonged in the kitchen—which things could go in the dishwasher, and exactly how to stack them. There were rules for everything, a place for everything.

So anal, my best friend from home would've said. But it was actually nice. The house where I'd grown up with my mom and brother and the string of men I was supposed to call *uncle* was full of junk, and you could never find anything you needed.

"That's kind of neat," I said, inspecting the silverware drawer. There was a tray inside, and the forks, spoons and knives were all separated out into their own little compartments.

"Something new and different?" Steele asked, amusement in his voice.

"Oh, yeah. We mostly grew up with plastic silverware. Tossed it straight in the trash when it was done."

His face darkened.

I stiffened. *Uh oh, I've said the wrong thing.*

"Such a waste," he said. "We need to look after this precious planet of ours. It's the only one we're going to get. I wish more people understood that."

"It's a real nice part of the planet here," I said quickly.

He nodded and the tension in his face eased away. "Most beautiful place on Earth. Come on, I'll show you around the ranch."

Then he stopped and gave me a hard look.

My breath caught in my throat.

What have I done now?

"Forgot about your clothes," he said. He strode to the mudroom, which led off the kitchen, and opened the dryer door. Squatting down, he fingered each of my items of clothing, while my stomach flip-flopped in embarrassment. "Almost done." He straightened up again. "You drink coffee?"

"I guess," I replied. I hated it actually, but didn't want him to think I was just a kid.

He raised a brow. "Another lie, young lady?"

I gulped. "No, sir. I don't like the taste, but I need the caffeine."

He seemed to accept that, and I let out a breath of relief. Maybe I'd keep calling him *sir* to butter him up. "I'll make a pot, then your clothes should be ready."

He had some fancy-looking machine. He showed me how to work it, "So you'll know for next time."

Before long, a rich aroma filled the kitchen, which smelled nothing like its bitter taste.

Steele handed me a cup. I sipped, focusing on keeping a straight face, but it was no good. My face automatically screwed up, and I shuddered.

Steele grinned. "I didn't like coffee until I was grown, either," he said. "And it taught me something important: some of the things you don't like at first end up being the things you come to appreciate the most."

Those narrow blue eyes lingered on me a beat too long, and I got the feeling he was referring to something completely different. All of a sudden, I got hot and shivery at the same time, and that bare place between my thighs started to tingle.

Was he saying he liked me?

No, that is ridiculous. Beyond ridiculous. No way would he be interested in someone like me.

I crossed my legs, desperate for my clothes to be dry.

Steele added some creamer and sugar to my cup and handed it back to me. "Try it like this, babygirl. Over time, you might find out you don't need as much creamer."

I sipped cautiously. The creamer was hazelnut flavor. "Not bad," I said.

He nodded, looking pleased, and warmth spread through my gut.

* * *

STEELE WENT OUT to the open fields and caught two horses—the one I'd made a giant fool of myself on earlier, and a smaller one with a shiny chestnut hide and a big round belly.

"Can't we walk instead?" I said, terrified at the thought of sitting in a saddle again.

He gave that dry laugh of his—which was more like a snort. "Not unless you want to be walking all night. There's a lot of land here." He slapped the horse's saddle. "Only thing to do when you've fallen off a horse is get right back on again."

"I tried that; you stopped me." I pouted at him. His mouth hovered between a frown and a smile, but the frown won out.

"That's right. You're not to try to ride Silver again without my say so. But this old girl will be just fine."

"B-but I can't," I stuttered, panic rising in my chest.

"Yes, you can. Now come on." He reached for my hand, enveloping it in his strong grasp, and drew me toward him.

"I'm scared. Can't I ride with you?"

His thumb rubbed the back of my hand, kinda like he was soothing me. "Not today, babygirl."

My cheeks flushed at his closeness. He seemed to realize what he'd said because he frowned and his voice hardened. "Enough of this, Carrie. Get on up."

I rolled my lips between my teeth. I was not faking my fear, and he seemed to realize that because he softened again.

"Poppy is real calm," he said. "I usually keep her for kids having their first riding lessons."

I kept protesting and his face hardened. "You agreed to

23

obey me. I'm telling you now, you disobey, you pay the price."

I wanted to dig in my heels, but could tell I'd pushed too far. "Fine." I put my foot in the stirrup and then he was helping me to swing my leg over Poppy's back.

"Okay?" He peered at me from under the brim of his hat, and I was startled by the concern in his eyes.

"Fine," I said, managing a small smile. He handed me the reins, and gave me a series of instructions. He was a natural teacher, I could tell. He took pleasure in sharing his wisdom and helping people.

"We're just going to walk," he assured me. "It's important to learn one gait at a time until you build confidence."

"Yes, sir." I mock saluted again and he frowned. Maybe he didn't like me calling him *sir*.

Poppy moved off slowly, following the big gray horse. It didn't feel so bad.

Keeping my attention on Steele helped me forget my nerves. I couldn't help thinking how sexy he looked on his horse, all rugged and wild. Like he was born to be on horseback, endlessly galloping across the plains... then coming back at night and making love to some lucky woman in front of an open fire.

The saddle rubbing between my legs must have me thinking this way.

The property was massive, stretching away toward the horizon. Low mountains rose in the distance. Where I was from, the land was flat, nothing to see. Here, the view took my breath away.

"Pretty, ain't it?" I said.

"Isn't it," Steele corrected, and I fought not to roll my eyes. "Yes, it is."

Half dude ranch, half beef farm, Steele explained. There

were eight luxury guest cabins, which were already closed up for the season.

"My brother Max manages that side of the business, while I take care of the horses and run the beef farm. We keep the two sides separate on purpose. Max and I are about as different as two brothers can be. Like chalk and cheese, my daddy always used to say. Max is the charming one—he loves entertaining. Has an eye for the ladies as well, especially the pretty female guests. He likes the city. I prefer the country. The fresh air and silence." The grooves beside Steele's mouth lessened as he looked across the land.

I cast an appreciative glance at him, thinking that was what I preferred, too.

"Watch out for Max," Steele said suddenly. "He's in the city at the moment, but he'll be back any day. He can be real persuasive sometimes. But he's not a one-woman guy, if you know what I mean?"

"Sure thing," I muttered, startled by the warning.

So he didn't just see me as a kid. He saw me as someone his brother might want to flirt with.

Did that mean he saw me that way, too?

We continued, passing through the middle of a cow field. Red and black Angus, he explained—premium beef cattle. I saw how the horses were unafraid of them, even when we passed two bulls that were busy butting heads. In the horse field, Steele pointed out some of the horses by name. He specialized in breaking horses that he'd either picked up at auction wild and unbroken, or ones that had been badly broken and had ended up damaged.

"There's not a lot you can't achieve through kindness and discipline," he commented.

Steele cared about the horses. He wanted to give them a better shot in life. I smiled to myself. Maybe this wouldn't be so bad.

"Sit up straight, Carrie," he reminded me. "Good posture will help you ride better."

"Yes, Mister Steele," I answered.

"Drop the *Mister*," he ordered.

"Yes, sir, Steele, sir," I said.

"Carrie." His tone carried a warning. I'd taken it too far. I didn't know what it was about him, but I was feeling cheeky.

"Is that why they call you Steele?" I asked as we rode on. "Because you're hard as steel?"

He ignored me, facing forward, his face stern.

I leaned forward. "Get it? 'Cause you're a hard ass?"

That did make him turn his head. "Watch your language," he said. "And mind your manners, or I'll turn you over my knee."

My eyes widened in shock. He gave me a glance that was pure heat. Was that amusement tucked in the corners of his mouth? Was he trying to flirt with me? If so, why did he threaten to spank me?

And why did the threat excite me?

Little butterflies fluttered in my gut as I settled back on the horse.

At the end of the ride, Steele took me to the stables where six horses were housed indoors. There were reasons why each one couldn't be in the field—either as part of the training process, or because they were recovering from injury. He showed me how to approach them, how to hold my hand out and let them sniff me first. I loved the warm breath from their nostrils, their huge dark eyes.

"This is Rex. Don't try to touch him. He's real wild, and mean as well." Steele indicated a big black stallion, who kept his back turned to us. His tail was filthy and matted, and his hide was covered in scars, like he'd come off the wrong side of a fight with a tiger.

"And this is our newest one." Steele indicated the horse in

the last stall. "Her name is Megan. She's just about broken now. She was nervous and flighty when I got her, but she's calmed down a lot." She was also a gray color but darker than Silver, with lighter gray spots on her rump, and a white mane and tail. When I stroked her velvety nose, she took a step forward and, to my delight, she nuzzled my neck. Right away, I decided she was my favorite.

"She likes you," Steele said thoughtfully.

When we'd finished with the horses, Steele showed me the cow he kept for milking.

"We milk her by hand—the old-fashioned way," he explained. "Just for our personal use, and any left over goes to our neighbors." The cow was mooing, her pink udders massively distended.

"Want to have a go?" Steele asked me. Then he frowned. He must have caught the look of disgust on my face. "Okay, not today. Guess it's a bit much for a city girl like you."

"I'm not a city girl—" I began to say, then cut myself off. I wasn't supposed to say anything about my background.

But if Steele noticed, he didn't say anything. Instead, he pulled out a small stool from the rear of the stable, put it down beside the big black-and-white cow, and began to pull on two of her long teats.

Soon, spurts of pure white milk began to fill a metal pail. It was kind of gross, but fascinating.

"Best milk you'll ever taste," he commented.

"Sure looks different from the stuff you get in a carton," I remarked.

He looked up at me and let his mouth soften into a grin, little creases appearing in the corners of his eyes.

"Welcome to the ranch," he said.

My heart filled with a sudden longing and I wished this could be my life, instead of a couple of days of living here until he kicked me out and I was on my own again.

* * *

NIGHT FELL FAST OUT THERE. I felt like I'd blinked and the sky become pure black velvet, twinkling with stars. It was about the most beautiful thing I'd ever seen. But with the darkness came my yawns. I was exhausted; I hadn't slept in a bed for days.

Back in the ranch house, Steele took a shower and changed into a pair of faded Levis and a navy T-shirt. There wasn't a spare inch of fat on him. He was all hard muscle, massive and honed from outdoor work. He looked softer now, the blue of the shirt enhancing the indigo of his eyes.

He heated up some stew on the stove, brushing away my offers of help. I went to set the table, and he clamped a hand on the back of my neck, guiding me to the table to sit down.

"Looks like you're just about to pass out, girlie," he said, and the look he gave me was kind.

I sat quietly until he served me, wondering at the tingling feeling where his fingers touched the back of my neck.

I ate fast, and since he didn't comment on my table manners, I figured he was going easy on me.

When I was done, he told me, "Go get your teeth brushed, then I'll show you to your sleeping quarters." His thick eyebrows drew together. "You have a toothbrush, right?"

"Of course," I scoffed.

Kind of weird to be questioned on my personal hygiene by a stranger, I thought as I brushed my teeth in front of the bathroom mirror. Especially since no one had ever cared if I brushed my teeth before. One more new thing in a whole day of new things.

Steele showed me to a barn behind the house. There was a basic bathroom in the corner, and up a ladder was a sleeping area with a mattress. He'd brought some blankets and fresh sheets, and watched critically while I put them on the mattress.

"You should be comfortable here," he said. "Now, I expect you up before dawn tomorrow—six a.m. Things start early around the ranch. Meet me at the door of the barn, and I'll assign your first task of the day. Understood?"

I nodded. "Understood," I repeated sleepily. I got under the blankets, and he bent over me and pulled them up to my chin. Something passed across his face as he straightened up again—something gentle. "You'll do just fine, here, girlie."

"Thank you," I murmured.

For a moment he looked like he'd say more, then he cleared his throat. "Sleep well, Carrie," he said as he descended the ladder.

I am safe, was my last thought that night. For the first time in weeks—in forever, actually. As strange as it seemed, I trusted this stern, handsome stranger, who woke me up in all kinds of ways.

I barely had time to switch off the lamp on the nightstand before I crashed out.

CHAPTER 3

Steele

$\mathcal{M}$y internal body clock woke me up at five-thirty a.m. the next morning, as it had every day for the past twenty-five years. I had no need for an alarm clock, even in the darkest days of winter.

It was pitch dark outside—still an hour from first light—and the mornings were getting chilly.

I pulled on a pair of jeans and a shirt, put on a pot of coffee, then went to check on the stabled horses, thinking all the time of the girl sleeping up in the barn. I hoped she'd been sleeping well, that whatever had made her run all the way up here wasn't invading her dreams.

She'd be warm enough up there for now. But when the season turned, it'd get too cold—

No. She was only staying for a couple of days. The last thing I needed this winter was to have a wild child to take care of, along with the horses and cows—not to mention my errant brother. He wanted out of the business. The ranch was our inheritance from my father, but Max wanted me to buy him out. He'd never wanted to be a cowboy. As soon as he turned eighteen, he started sneaking off to the city at every opportunity. I'd spent a couple of years in Vancouver, too, trying it on for size. But my heart would always be here, in the wide open plains, surrounded by my horses.

The trouble was, the business wasn't currently earning enough for me to purchase Max's half, and our relationship was getting more acrimonious by the day. Good job he was away at the moment—he'd take one look at Carrie, and decide he was going to eat her for breakfast. I was pretty sure she had no idea how sexy she was. She was streetwise and troubled, yes, but underneath that was an innocence. And there was no way in hell I was going to let my brother corrupt it.

The sooner Carrie was out of here, the better. I'd let her stay a couple of days, just long enough to figure out what had scared her so badly. I was worried about her—worried that she was mixed up in something bad. My instinct was to drag it out of her, but she was skittish enough to run if I pushed her too hard. I needed to tease it out of her, then I'd set her on the right track and send her off on her way.

The sooner she was gone, the better. I didn't need the feelings she stirred up.

The horses nickered in greeting, blowing clouds of condensation through their nostrils. I patted each one, checking up on them as they pushed their noses into my hand with their horsey curiosity. I usually fed them now, but I'd leave that as a treat for Carrie after she'd finished her tasks. She'd like that.

I checked my watch. It was five-fifty a.m. and no light was showing from the upper floor of the barn. I grabbed a rake and cleaned up the dead leaves around the trees in the yard.

Another job I'd been planning to leave for Carrie, but I could never sit around idle when there was work to be done.

Five fifty-nine a.m.—and still no sign of the wayward girl. I went into the kitchen, and poured another cup of coffee.

Ten minutes I'd give her, I told myself, my fingers flexing.

I didn't usually go so easy on my new recruits. Most of them got a rude awakening on day one. Especially the ones who thought they could laze about for twenty-two hours a day, pull off a couple hours' work whenever they rolled out of bed, and expected me to feed them and give them a roof over their heads. But she'd been exhausted yesterday, poor thing. She'd barely had the energy to finish her dinner.

If she were mine, there'd be no need for an alarm clock. I'd wake her up with my mouth between her legs. Tease her to the brink of climax and back off, again and again, until she was begging me. Then I'd pull her into the shower and put her on her knees so she could suck me off before bending her over and pounding her to climax.

For the first few months with a submissive, I had the stamina of a twenty something. But with Carrie, I'd bet it would be years before the edge wore off.

I checked the clock. Six-fifteen a.m.—still no sign of Carrie. And thanks to my fool thoughts, now I was hard as iron with no chance for relief.

Annoyance bubbled in my veins. Carrie wasn't my sub, she was my ranch hand. I needed to stop giving her special treatment, even if it went against every protective instinct I had.

I strode over to the barn, and flicked on the light switch on the ground floor.

"Wake up," I called. I listened for the usual groans and murmured apologies.

Nothing.

"Wake up, Carrie," I shouted, much sterner this time.

33

Still nothing.

My palms began to itch. I went over to the foot of the ladder. "Don't make me come up for you, young lady!" I growled.

What insolence! I shook my head. She was about to learn she wasn't going to get away with this type of behavior. I climbed the ladder, the structure trembling under my weight.

Then I stopped dead. There was no sign of her. The blanket was spread lumpily across the bed. She'd left already.

Disappointment sat heavy in my gut. It turned out I hadn't wanted her to leave after all.

Then I caught a small movement beneath the covers.

Somehow, she was under there. And she hadn't even woken up. I grabbed the corner of the coverlet and yanked it off.

She was curled up on her side, fully dressed in her jeans and T-shirt, her straw-colored hair all mussed. She looked adorable. The sight was like waving a red flag in front of a bull.

I had to step back to get a hold of myself.

Her eyes flickered open. "What time is it?" she mumbled in a voice thick with sleep.

"Time you got up, girlie." My cock was about to punch through my jeans.

Her eyes widened. "B-but—" she stammered, groping for her phone, which I saw was on the wooden crate that served as a nightstand. She looked at the screen and sighed.

"Thought I set the alarm," she mumbled.

"Doesn't look like it." I crossed my arms over my chest. I had to be firm. If she was going to stay on the farm, she had to pull her weight.

She looked over to the window confusedly. "It's still dark outside. It's not late."

"There's plenty of work to do before it gets light," I said.

"And I'm not waiting around for lazy workers who think they can take advantage of me." That was all she was. A ranch hand.

She rubbed her eyes. Her lower lip puffed out in a familiar pout. "What's the big deal, anyway? Your ad said five hours' work a day. It's like the middle of the night. There's plenty of time to get five hours' work done today, I'm sure." Carrie blinked up at me, looking sweet and virginal. She caught a glimpse of my angry face, and her green eyes widened. Her tongue darted out to lick her lips, and my cock thickened even more. Victoria used to try those tricks. I'd let them work before, but not anymore.

I made my voice hard as steel. "Get yourself up and get down that ladder, right now. And bring your things with you."

She blinked. "You're kicking me out?"

"I haven't decided what I'm going to do with you." I stalked down the ladder, my anger growing with every step. She was late, and she didn't even give a damn about it. Worse, her presence made me painfully aroused.

I needed to remember she wasn't my sub. But if she was a real ranch worker, she'd be gone by now.

Carrie followed me down the ladder, that grubby backpack of hers slung over her shoulder, and her hair still tangled like a rat's nest. Now she looked less sure of herself.

"Can I at least go pee?" she mumbled.

I nodded. "Yeah, go get washed up and fix your hair—it looks like a haystack. I'll see you back here in ten minutes."

She scuttled off to the bathroom, and I walked a couple of loops around the house to calm my temper.

I couldn't abide such sassy, childish behavior. It was the kind of thing I'd punish a sub for.

She wasn't a bad kid, but she hadn't had an iota of discipline in her short life—that much was obvious.

What the hell was I going to do with her?

My thoughts flipped back and forth.

On one hand was the possibility of Carrie staying with me a few days longer. On the other was me kicking her out on her ass.

And in the middle...

In the middle was a place I'd gone before. My favorite place. It'd be new to Carrie, but I could see her through it. Maybe we could both enjoy it.

Yesterday, I'd concluded that what she needed was a firm hand. I'd tried to treat her like another ranch hand, and it wasn't working. She stirred every protective instinct I had—and more. Darker, baser desires.

And I was done denying myself.

Carrie emerged from the bathroom at last. She jerked her chin up when she saw me, still more defiant than apologetic. She wasn't afraid of me—that was a good sign.

I hitched my thumbs in my jeans and glared down at her. "You going to apologize now?"

She shrugged. "Sure."

I took a step toward her, so she was forced to tilt her head back to look up at me. "That's not an apology."

She sighed. "I don't get what the big deal is, anyway. It's still dark as shit out there."

"Language," I barked, and she jumped. I waited for an apology and she pressed her lips together.

Strike two.

"The big deal is, Carrie, I gave you an instruction and you failed to carry it out."

"But I'm here now. You could've hollered for me."

"I did holler for you. And you've got a phone to wake you up."

"The battery died."

I clenched my teeth. "You're about the thirtieth traveler

36

I've had here. All the good ones got up when I told them to, worked a few hours in the morning, then had most of the day to themselves. Riding horses, whatever they wanted. I've got no time for little girls who want to lie in bed all day."

"I'm not a little girl." Carrie looked mutinous.

"You're acting like one."

"Can't you just chill out? You said the season's over, anyway. I mean, lighten up, already." She raised her small shoulders in a nonchalant shrug.

"That's it, young lady. I told you, if you didn't obey, there'd be consequences." I grabbed her by the wrist and pulled her toward me.

"What are you doing?" She fought to get away, but I held her firmly by both arms.

The idea crystallized in my mind, fizzed in my blood. It energized every cell of my body, leaving my palms tingling in anticipation.

"You agreed to abide by the rules. And if you agreed if you broke them, you'd pay the price. Now it's time to pay up and take your punishment," I said.

Her pale green eyes got very wide. "Wh-what?"

"I'm going to punish you," I said. "You've been very disobedient. And if there's one thing I can't tolerate, it's disobedience."

She scoffed. "Punish me? What are you talking about?"

I swallowed hard, pushing back on the mixture of emotions racing through my body. "I'm going to spank your behind."

Her mouth fell open. "No. No way." Again, she scrabbled again to get away from me, like a cat caught in a net, and this time, I let her go.

"Leave then. Your choice. I didn't give you a chance yesterday so that you could take advantage of me at the very first turn."

I strode over to a hay bale at the side of the room and sat down, planting my legs wide apart.

"It's my way or nothing, babygirl. You either take your jeans down and lie across my lap, or you get your stuff and leave."

She stood in the middle of the barn and stared at me, arms folded. "No," she repeated. "Not happening."

"Your choice, Carrie. I'm giving you one minute to make your mind up."

CHAPTER 4

Carrie

I stared and stared at Steele in disbelief. Sitting there on the hay bale, legs apart.

Waiting for me.

He has to be kidding, right? This is just some weird joke of his.

But the expression on his face said different. Those narrow, blue eyes bored into mine, uncompromising. Pitiless.

Subconsciously, my hands drifted to my ass cheeks. He really wanted to *spank* me? I couldn't believe my ears. Spankings were for little girls, not full-grown adults. Not employees. My mouth almost fell open. It sounded so crazy, it was almost funny.

"Thirty seconds, Carrie," Steele barked. "Your decision."

My eyes snapped from his big, denim-clad thighs to his face, and back again. He wasn't kidding. He really was going to kick me out if I didn't agree to this.

I guess I understood why he was mad—I shouldn't have overslept, but I really hadn't thought it was such a big deal. Maybe I deserved some kind of punishment. *Like—I don't know—having to shovel an extra pile of horse shit or something.*

But physical punishment? On my ass? I'd likely been spanked as a small child, but I couldn't really remember. But as an adult? That idea just about blew my mind.

"Ten seconds, Carrie." Steele's voice cut through my circling thoughts, harsh and unforgiving.

I turned and glanced through the barn door at the outdoors—at the dull gray light that was beginning to chase away the dark. Either I walked out into that, into nowhere. *Or*, I allowed Steele to spank me on my bare ass.

What a choice to have to make. I bit down on my lower lip; twisted my hands together. Why was I so excited?

"Carrie?" There was a warning tone in Steele's voice now.

I swallowed hard. *Aw, hell.*

I walked over to him with slow, dragging steps, coming to a stop three feet away. Head spinning, stomach squirming, I looked at him expectantly.

His gaze dropped to the zipper of my jeans, and he gave a curt nod.

A blast of excitement went right through me, leaving my hairs standing on end. I put my hands on the button, and hesitated.

"I'm not going to do anything inappropriate, Carrie. I just want to make sure you feel your punishment." Steele's voice was softer now.

Slowly, slowly, I unfastened the button and eased down the zipper. My cheeks burned with embarrassment but my stomach flip flopped. Not with fear, but anticipation.

Steele's eyes raked over my hips and, as if they were laser beams guiding me, I eased my jeans down to thigh level. Now he could see my panties, which were pink with roses on. More childish than sexy, but I'd picked them up cheap in a supermarket somewhere. I hated the fact that he was seeing them. He probably thought I was a little girl—as if he didn't already.

Now, he brought his knees together and beckoned with his hand. "Come over here."

My skin tingling with embarrassment and apprehension, I shuffled over to his right side, then bent forward awkwardly until my hands came to rest on his thigh. I could feel the warmth of his skin through his jeans, the bulky muscles beneath.

"Put your weight on me," he told me, and took hold of my waist, guiding me across his lap. I had no choice but to let my weight fall onto him.

Yuck. This felt very weird.

Then he raised his right leg, and tipped me. I lurched forward and let out a yelp. My feet scrabbled for purchase on the wooden floorboards, but I was unbalanced, dangling perilously across his lap.

"Shush," he murmured. "Don't worry about anything." When he laid his hand on my ass, I squeaked. It was half on my panties, and half on my bare skin. He tapped my right cheek and then my left.

"You'll feel better after this," he told me. "This is what you need."

"No one needs their ass whupping—" I started to say, but there was a whoosh, then a crack as a heavier slap landed on my right cheek.

"Ouch!" I yelled, more in surprise than pain.

"Shush," he said again, like he was calming a flighty animal. I heard him breathing, slow and deep, several times, like he was psyching himself up for something.

There was a pause, that whoosh again, and another *slap!* landed, this time on my left cheek.

It stung. I let out a yelp, and wriggled to get away, but I was held fast over his lap, kicking my legs uselessly.

"Please," I cried out. "I'll be good."

His large palm soothed my bottom. "I know you will, babygirl." The fight went out of me at the warmth in his voice. His fingers continued to rub my ass. "You need discipline. It's okay, baby, I'll give you what you need. Hold still, it'll be over soon."

There was another slap on my right cheek, exactly where the first one had been.

I yelped again at the sting. A fourth one fell on the left side again. Then a storm of stinging slaps rained down—left, then right, higher then lower—until my entire ass had been covered by his palm. The slaps rang out in between my cries. It *hurt*.

But when he stopped to rub my butt again, the stinging went away, swallowed up by the ache between my legs.

"You take your punishment like a good girl, and then it'll be over. You'll be forgiven." His murmur made me melt. "You understand?"

"Yes," I whispered.

A few more slaps, and I gritted my teeth and took them quietly.

"That's it." He paused, his hand caressing my ass over my panties. Relief swept through me. *He's done. Thank goodness.*

"I want you to count for me," he said.

"Wh-what?" I mumbled.

"I'm going to give you twenty."

I went ramrod stiff. *Going to* give me?

"What about the ones you've given me already?" I yelped.

"Those were just the warm up," he said. "Now, *this* is your punishment for disrespecting me."

Crack! A much harder slap landed on my left cheek, right on the spot where my ass met my thigh. It burned like crazy, and I yowled like a cat that'd had its tail trodden on. "Shit!"

Steele went still. Long enough that I lifted my head. "I told you to count," he said in a hard voice. "If you don't do exactly what I tell you, these panties of yours are coming down as well." He hooked his finger in the elastic of the waistband and snapped it.

Alarm jolted through me. "One," I muttered.

Steele grabbed hold of the waistband and tugged downward.

"One," I said, in a much clearer voice.

"Good," he said.

Crack! His hand came down on my right cheek.

"Two!" I shouted out.

Crack, crack, crack!

His hand came down heavily, each slap in a different place from the last. Soon, my entire ass was on fire. I could feel it radiating heat, and hated to think he could see it turning red.

How shameful.

"Seven! Eight! Nine!"

The numbers burst from my lips.

The tenth one was hard to take. The eleventh was unbearable. I wriggled on his lap, trying to predict where the next one would land, desperate to escape the relentless rhythm of his hand.

"Hold still," he told me again. "The more you cooperate, the quicker it'll be over."

I wrapped my arm around his denim-clad thigh. Somehow, the smell of his laundry powder gave me a scrap of comfort amid all this suffering.

Sixteen... seventeen... eighteen. I couldn't stand it. Wild, humiliating sounds spilled from my mouth, and I squeezed my eyes shut, tears threatening.

"Nineteen!" I yelled in a ragged voice, and, "Twenty" was a sob, tears finally running down my cheeks.

Then it all stopped. There was quiet. I went limp across Steele's lap.

My body was shuddering all over. My throat hurt; my ass felt hot enough to fry eggs on. But, most shamefully of all, there was a deep, pulsing ache between my thighs.

Somewhere, in the midst of all that pain and humiliation, I'd gotten turned on. I'd felt it before the real punishment had even started. As much as I'd flinched at every blow, I'd also *kind of* hoped for it. *What is wrong with me?*

Steele's hand came down again, and I flinched. But this time, he touched me lightly. He made circles with a featherlight touch, easing the throbbing of my bruised flesh. My skin was so sensitized that I could feel the coarseness of his fingertips.

"There, there," he murmured. "All done now. You are such a good girl."

Good girl. The praise lit something in me, but I frowned and fought it. I was shaky with emotion, and my butt was sore. There was no reason for me to feel so good.

"You can get up now," he said. He tipped me back until my feet could touch the floor again, and awkwardly, I pushed back on his thighs until I was standing up. As I pulled up my jeans, I felt the moisture pooling between my thighs. I kept my eyes on the ground, my face as hot as my ass.

"Now, Carrie, I hope you've learned your lesson. I would hate to have to do that again."

I looked up at him. His expression was calm. I ducked my head, letting my hair fall over my face.

"Have you?" he pressed me.

"Yes." I nodded vigorously, worried that he might think about going for another round.

His lips formed an uncompromising line. "Then thank me for your punishment."

My mouth fell open. "What—" I started to say, until the warning look in his eyes cut me off.

I swallowed hard.

"Thank you for punishing me for my disobedience," I said. Even as the words left my mouth, I couldn't believe I'd just uttered them. I felt dizzy, like I'd just stepped into an alternate universe.

"Good girl." He patted the hay bale next to him. "Take a seat."

I sat down, and he rubbed my back in big, comforting circles while I tried not to sniffle.

"How are you feeling?" he asked.

Angry, I was about to say, but that wasn't the truth. The truth was more complicated, and I didn't yet have the words for it.

"Okay, I guess," I mumbled instead.

"I think that did you a lot of good," he said in a low voice. "It might not make sense right now, but in time it will, I promise."

My mouth opened and closed several times, but no sound came out.

"I'll go get your cup of coffee." He disappeared out of the barn, leaving me alone with my thoughts.

CHAPTER 5

Carrie

*M*y ass was still throbbing and it was uncomfortable to sit down. I would have got to my feet except my legs didn't feel strong enough to hold me up.

Steele whupping my ass was supposed to do me good?

That was some fucked up shit.

And yet, my pussy was burning with need. That had been the weirdest, most humiliating, most arousing experience of my entire life.

If he came back and started to kiss me, I knew I wouldn't stop him. I was still a virgin, but I still wouldn't stop him from pulling off my clothes and taking me right there in the hay. I imagined him naked, his huge body on top of me. His cock inside me. How would it feel? He was too big and rough and old for me. But my traitorous body tingled with yearning.

The door banged, and Steele was back with the coffee. I watched him striding toward me with his loose, confident gait. My eyes zeroed in on his crotch. I wondered if it had turned him on to smack my ass, or if it'd only been about punishment for him.

Was it supposed to be sexual? Was it weird that I'd gotten turned on?

I felt awkward as he approached, like I didn't know how to act around him. I wound up jamming my hands in my pockets, and staring at the floor.

"Here." He handed me a steaming earthenware mug. I wrapped my hands around it. The warmth was comforting. I wished he'd rub my back again.

"I put an extra spoon of sugar in it. Think you'll appreciate it," he commented, blowing on his own black brew.

"Thanks," I mumbled, still too uncomfortable to look him in the eye.

He was right. When the sugar reached my blood, that nervous shaky feeling left my body.

"You all right?" He bumped his arm against mine. I nodded.

All right was not the expression for whatever I was feeling right now. Confused. Freaked out. Disturbed. About two seconds away from grabbing my bag and running all the way back to the station, however long it took me.

I sensed his eyes burning into me but I kept my chin tucked down, eyes on the ground.

"C'mere." He took the cup out of my hand and set it on the floor, and I was suddenly enfolded in his huge arms. He pressed my head against his chest, the buttons of his shirt chafing my cheek.

I wanted to fight him, but instead a weird hiccup burst out of my mouth and I found myself leaning into him, letting my body go limp. He stroked my hair soothingly, and my nostrils filled with that exciting, spicy scent of his.

"All better now," he said, his deep voice vibrating through his chest.

I drew in some long breaths. They shuddered in my throat, sounding like a child when it's been sobbing for a long time and is all cried out. There *was* a sense of relief in my body—as though I'd healed from something. Strangely, I felt drowsy.

Just as my eyelids were getting heavy, Steele pulled away.

I blinked, already missing the warmth of his body. I should've hated him, but instead, all I wanted was for him to hold me a little bit longer.

He gave me a lingering look, then handed me the cup again. "Drink up, and I'll show you how to muck out the stables. Then we'll have breakfast."

Obediently, I took the mugs indoors and put them in the dishwasher, then followed Steele to the stables.

I watched dazedly as he led the first horse—a huge, sleek black one—out of the stall and tied it to a fence rail. It was lively, tossing its head and dancing like it was desperate to go join its friends in the field. It was beautiful, but I was a little afraid of its massive, muscular body and dangerous-looking hooves.

"Maybe you can start leading them out tomorrow," Steele told me. I looked at the horse doubtfully. It looked like it could run off with me dangling off the end of the rope.

Steele caught my expression and chuckled. He stroked the horse's nose and ears, and it lowered its head. "You see it as a dangerous animal, but it doesn't think of itself like that. A horse is a prey animal. Easily scared. You master it with a kind but firm touch. You teach it to trust you, and it doesn't think about kicking you anymore."

He looked at me significantly as he spoke, and I had the strangest feeling he was actually talking about me.

Whatever. If he thought he was going to tame me like a wild beast, he had another think coming.

He took out a brush and began to groom the horse. I watched, grudgingly at first.

It was kind of fascinating the way this gruff, intimidating guy turned gentle. He brushed the animal's shiny hide all over, then its legs, and it lifted up its feet so he could scrape out its hooves with a curved tool. Then he took a different comb and brushed out its mane and tail. I got a weird feeling in my stomach that was a bit like envy.

Idiot. Who gets jealous over a horse?

Probably someone who'd never had their hair brushed by anyone else in their life.

"Okay, done," Steele said with satisfaction. "Now I'll show you how to get the stable cleaned up."

He grabbed a broom and a shovel and showed me his technique, and I got to work.

My arms felt weak because I hadn't had breakfast yet, but I tried my best, wanting him to be pleased with me.

As I worked, I was aware of that dampness between my thighs, sticky and distracting. And every time I glanced up at Steele, it only got worse.

I wanted him more since he'd spanked me. *How screwed up is that?* I wanted him to kiss me, take my clothes off, touch me all over.

More than touch me.

Like he'd be into me, anyway. I was just a teen. He hadn't even believed I was over eighteen, while he had to be at least forty. He said he didn't have a wife, but maybe he was divorced. There's no way a man as hot as Steele would be single. He probably had a girlfriend somewhere.

I conjured up an image of her in my mind. She'd be real

classy, but not afraid to get her hands dirty. She probably wore tailored shirts from some designer store, and kept her hair nice, in long, dark curls. She'd look at me and laugh at the thought I had a crush on her sexy man.

I glanced at Steele yet again. He happened to look up at the same moment, and our eyes met. My cheeks burning, I dropped my gaze to the ground.

When I'd piled all the mess into a wheelbarrow, Steele showed me how to spread a layer of clean straw across the floor. Then we filled up the feeding trough with hay. The horse was eager to go back into its stable, pricking up its ears and sniffing around curiously.

We repeated the process with the next stable, Steele taking the horse out to groom it while I mucked out.

We didn't speak much, but I kept sneaking glances at him when he wasn't looking, watching the concentration on his handsome face, the way the muscles in his bare forearms flexed as he tended to the horses with such skill and kindness.

Finally, we were done. It was fully light by now. I'd missed seeing the sun rise and it was already high in the sky, partly hidden by hazy orange clouds. Steele told me to take the full wheelbarrow out to a manure heap at the back. It didn't smell as bad as I'd expected. But on the way back, I discovered I was sweating all over, gross damp patches under my arms. Mucking out was hot work.

I was surprised when Steele let us walk into the kitchen in our horsey-smelling clothes.

"We'll get washed up later," he said, with his eerie habit of knowing exactly what I was thinking. "Time for breakfast first."

My stomach rumbled again. "Sorry," I mumbled, feeling childish.

"Sign you've worked up an appetite," he said, and his eyes crinkled at the corners like he thought I was charming.

This time, he made me his assistant in the kitchen, giving me instructions on how to set everything up. We were having eggs and bacon, and since that was one of the few things I knew how to cook, I volunteered to take over.

Steele hovered beside me, and I could practically see the tension crackling off him. But when the food was ready, he nodded appreciatively. "Good work, girlie," he said, and a silly glow of pride warmed me through.

I set everything up on the table—fork on the left, knife on the right—then we dug in.

When we were done, Steele prepared to check on the cows. "Go get showered now," he told me. "See that you're ready by the time I'm back, then I've got someplace to take you."

I got ready as quickly as I could, wondering what he had in mind. My jeans stank of horses. It wasn't a bad smell really, but I figured other folks wouldn't appreciate it, so I put on my shorts. Then I washed up the breakfast things. It was kind of nice having the place all tidy, the sink clear of dirty dishes.

Soon, Steele strode back in, whistling to himself. "All good," he said. "Three calves were born in the night, and they're all fine."

"Can I see them sometime?" I asked him.

"Sure thing." He nodded, looking pleased. Fireworks went off in my bloodstream and I grinned back, full of a giddy feeling.

Steele had one of those intimidating Ford pickups, all gleaming black with a mean-looking grill.

"You going to tell me where we're going?" I asked as we set off, getting frustrated with his secretiveness.

"You'll see," was his only reply.

But when we passed a sign for the town, alarm spiked in my chest.

"You're not taking to me to the station?" I demanded, sounding surly to hide my fear.

He started to frown at my tone. But when he caught the look on my face, it died away.

"No, of course not. What got that idea into your head? We're going shopping—figured you needed some new clothes."

"Shopping?" I echoed stupidly. "But I don't have any—"

"Don't worry about that," he cut in. "Think I can stretch to a couple of sets of clothes. And you did good today."

I stared out of the windshield, kind of confused. He had a point though—my wardrobe needed a refresh in a big way. I'd left my home so fast, I'd only had time to grab the first things I put my hands on. Steele had noticed, and he cared, like no one ever had before. It made me feel warm to my toes.

Before long, we arrived in Ashcroft. It was a quaint country town—wide roads and long, low buildings. It reminded me of my hometown, but it was a lot prettier.

Steele pulled into the parking lot of Hoyle's department store. As we walked across the lot, several people called out greetings to him. I got the impression he was well-known and liked around here.

The store was old-fashioned, but it had a homely feel, and I liked it.

Steele strode through the different departments like a man on a mission, and I trotted at his side, doing my best to keep up with his loping gait. We passed through the home improvement and kitchen departments before arriving at the women's fashion section.

Immediately, he began to go through the clothing rails, like he'd done it a hundred times before.

"How about these?" he said, handing me a couple of pairs of jeans. "And these…" He added some shirts to the pile, and then a couple of wifebeaters, and a sweater. Apparently, he was in charge of picking my clothes out, and I was happy enough for him to do it—I would've been too embarrassed to do it myself. Before long, my arms were full, but he kept going, getting more enthusiastic the more stuff he found.

Finally, he stopped and looked at me seriously, eyes narrowed. "Guess you'll be needing some new underthings, too?"

I froze; my breath caught in my lungs. "Guess so," I managed to croak.

When we approached the underwear section, he seemed a little less confident. "You should probably choose your own," he muttered. "I don't know about this kind of thing."

A hot wave of embarrassment washed over me. Was he really going to stand here and watch me pick out underwear?

Apparently, he was. He took the pile of clothes from me and stood at my side as I deliberated over a multipack of patterned cotton panties, and some fancier ones that were displayed on individual hangers. I lifted my hand and fingered a pair of cream lace panties. They were the kind I liked to wear best.

"You should get those," Steele muttered. His voice was a little hoarse, like he had something stuck in his throat.

"Okay," I said, and snatched them up.

"And maybe the matching brassiere." He jabbed a finger at the row of bras above.

My cheeks heating, I rummaged through until I found my size. I was a B cup; wished I was a C.

Jeez, this was more embarrassing than the time I'd asked my mom to take me bra shopping, but in a totally different way. Was he imagining what I'd look like in this underwear set? I didn't think he was into me, but still, he was a guy…

No, there was no way he would see me as anything but a homeless runaway. A girl to be pitied. He could crook his finger, and any woman would come running. Why would he want me?

"Okay, think I'm ready," I blurted out. Keeping my head down, I looked around for the changing room.

Steele followed me, but to my relief, he sat outside on one of the chairs that seemed to have been put out for guys accompanying their partners on shopping trips.

I went in and started trying stuff on. Steele had done a good job of guessing my size, and I put everything into two piles—a big pile of stuff that fit, and a smaller one of stuff that didn't.

And then, at the bottom of the pile was a dress. I held it up, squinting under the garish store lights.

It was dusky pink, with a lace panel on the front and capped sleeves. The skirt was full and came out from a high waist. Not my usual taste, but pretty. Couldn't hurt to try it on, I guessed.

I slithered into it and zipped it up. It actually fit perfectly, enhancing the shape of my skinny body. It made me look older, more sophisticated.

"Need any help in there?" Steele's deep voice came from the other side of the curtain.

I jumped. "Th-there's a dress here. I don't know where it came from—"

"Let me see." Before I could argue, he yanked the curtain wide open.

Then he stood very still. His lips parted, and his irises turned from cornflower blue to deep navy.

"You look very pretty," he said at last. His tone was low, gravelly, and it sent shivers right through me.

"I was just trying it on." I smoothed the skirt self-consciously.

"You're taking it," he said.

I opened my mouth to say I couldn't, but he had that uncompromising set to his jaw again. I nodded. "Thank you," I said in a small voice.

"Everything else fit?"

I pointed to the big pile. "All this."

"Hand it to me, and bring the dress out when you're done."

I fingered the fabric. I felt different wearing the dress. Beautiful. But I couldn't possibly afford it. "No—I—it's too much. I have no way of paying you back."

"Do as you're told, babygirl." He slid the curtain shut, and he was gone.

I changed back into my old T-shirt and shorts, tingling all over. No one had taken me shopping like this before. When I was growing up, most of my clothes had come from Goodwill. But Steele—my new employer—was taking care of me like this. Buying me all these gifts. It was too much for my brain to handle.

When I emerged from the changing room, he was waiting for me. He took the dress with a businesslike smile and marched up to the sales desk. I trailed after him, hands stuffed into my pockets. We were getting some curious glances from the customers and the cashier, but Steele seemed oblivious to them. He was humming to himself and making conversation with the cashier like he was having a real good day. He was pleased with me, and I liked that feeling.

Outside, I walked alongside him feeling like a little girl on her birthday—no, more like a grown woman with an adoring boyfriend or husband. I was proud to be seen at his side, and hoped people would think we were together. It was a giddy, special feeling, and I wanted to enjoy it for as long as possible.

Instead of heading back to the truck, we crossed the lot and turned onto the sidewalk.

"Where we going?" I asked.

"If you're going to be riding horses, you need real boots," was the answer. He put a hand on my back. "Stand up straight, Carrie," he ordered. "You're slouching."

"More rules," I muttered, but did as I was told.

Steele led me to an old-fashioned shoe shop and held the door for me to go inside. There was a strong smell of new leather, and inside were rows of boots designed for outdoor living.

Sitting by the cashier's desk was a guy in a vest, with a big droopy moustache. He greeted Steele warmly.

"How you doing, Carl?" Steele said. "Need a special pair of boots for the young lady."

Carl's eyes lit up. "I've got just the pair," he said. "What size?"

I told him, and he disappeared in the back and returned with a pair of boots in a box. They were beautiful—brown leather on the shoe part, and embroidered teal leather going up the leg.

Steele told me to take a seat on a leather bench, and I tried to pull the boots on. They were tight as hell. I grunted and strained, but they wouldn't budge past my instep.

"That's how they're supposed to be when you first get them," he remarked. Then he went behind me, reached around my back, and tugged with both hands. Suddenly he was all wrapped around, his torso pressing up against my back and his stubble brushing my cheek. I couldn't breathe. I forgot I was supposed to be helping him. All I was aware of was his scent surrounding me, his big, hard body encircling me.

At last, my heel popped into the boot. Steele released me

and I staggered to my feet and walked around. The shoes fit but my toes were pinched.

"They'll take a bit of wearing in," Steele commented. "But when you get used to them, you'll never want to take them off."

I glanced at Steele's dark brown boots, which were battered from years of hard wear. What was that thing about a cowboy keeping his boots on even in bed? Suddenly, an image of Steele in nothing but his boots burst into my mind. A little tingle started up between my thighs and I turned away from him fast, before my face started to burn as well.

"You'll need some feminine shoes, too," Steele said, striding around the small shop, surveying the stock. "How about these?" He pointed to a pair of black patent Mary Janes.

I opened my mouth to make some comment about just how unhip they were. Then I shut it again. "They're pretty," I said instead.

Carl brought over a pair of size sixes and I tried them on. They didn't look so bad when they were on my feet. They'll go nicely with the dress," Steele said, and I was glad if that made him happy.

"Okay, that'll be $365," Carl said, ringing everything up in the cash register.

I gaped. I'd had no idea cowboy boots were so expensive. But Steele handed over his credit card like he bought expensive gifts for his ranch hands every day.

"You like ice cream?" he asked once we strolling along the sidewalk again.

"Sure," I replied.

We passed down a side street and through the door of an old-style creamery. It had white tiles on the walls and fancy gold writing on the windows.

"This place opened up a while ago—I've been looking for an excuse to try it out," he explained gruffly.

I eyed him sideways. "Guess I'm *an excuse?*"

"Yep." His expression didn't change, but I sensed his smile.

The store had all kinds of hip flavors like lavender and rose petal. I ordered one scoop of pistachio and one of rose petal, but Steele looked perturbed by the selection.

He wasn't a guy for fancy flavors, apparently.

"You like vanilla bean?" I asked him.

"Yup," he said.

"And chocolate?"

He nodded thoughtfully. "Happens to be my favorite."

"You have plain chocolate?" I asked the woman at the counter.

"I think we have some out the back," she said.

Steele threw me a look of gratitude and I was glad I could do something for him, however small.

We took a table at the window and I felt his eyes scanning me appreciatively while I took tiny licks of the ice cream. He was pleased with me, and I liked that feeling.

The lighting in the shop was dim, and late-afternoon light glowed through the windows. It felt so nice being here with him; so normal. But the more normal it seemed, the more I felt like I was the odd one out in this scene. I didn't belong here, not with the ugly secret that trailed behind me. I started to feel confused and panicky.

"What is it, Carrie?" Steele was looking at me with concern.

"Why are you doing all this?" I blurted out.

His eyebrows dropped down low. "Doing what?"

"All this... this... taking care of me, buying me things. I mean, I'll be gone in a few days..." I broke off, my throat tight, already feeling the tug of separation.

Steele looked at me like he was weighing up what to say.

"Do you want to be gone in a few days?" he said at last.

I gazed at him wordlessly, thinking—about everything I had run from. About the fear that had filled my every thought for the past days. I felt safe with Steele—as crazy as that sounded. I barely knew him, and I'd already let him spank my bare ass. And he intimidated the hell out of me.

But I sensed that he had a good heart. He made me want to be better.

And... my attraction to him was getting out of control.

I swallowed hard. "No. I don't."

His expression got even more serious. "You haven't had much order in your life—that's not your fault. I'll make an educated guess you haven't had a lot of care, either."

I stared at him, unblinking, but the back of my eyes began to prickle.

"You need a firm hand," he continued. "That's very obvious to me. I'm pretty sure you're not telling me everything, and I'm not comfortable with that. But you can stay with me, as long as you—" he paused and scratched at his stubble, "submit to my discipline." He fixed me with an unwavering gaze.

Discipline.

The sound of that word in Steele's deep voice—

I was damned if that little tingle didn't start up between my thighs again.

I swallowed. "You mean—" I couldn't bring myself to say the words.

He nodded. "I will punish you when you do wrong. Give you guidance on the right way to do things. Teach you that order will bring happiness and meaning to your life."

"P-punish me like you did today?" I stammered.

He gave another deep nod. "With my hand. With my belt, if you need it. And any other way I deem appropriate."

My eyes flickered from his big hand to the chunky leather belt that was fitted through his belt loops. And that tingle between my thighs bloomed into a deep, throbbing ache.

Shame and arousal washed through me in waves. *Bed and board in exchange for getting my ass whupped? What am I agreeing to?*

But getting to stay with Steele… letting him take my jeans down… feeling his hand on my bare flesh.

"Breathe, babygirl," he murmured. "And sit up straight. You're slouching again."

I made my back straight as a board. Steele's eyes glittered. He was so bossy—and now I knew why.

"You probably need some time to think about it," he continued. "I understand if you're scared."

"I'm not scared. It's just… different." I took a big lick of my ice cream before it dripped onto my hand. Steele watched me intently. And I loved that.

"There's something here. I'd like to explore it," he said. "But I understand if you need time—"

"No. I've decided—I want to stay with you," I said quietly.

"And you agree to my *terms*?"

My cheeks heated again and my stomach did a flip.

"That I can disci—"

"Yes," I said quickly, before he had time to say that humiliating word again. "I agree to your terms."

"Good," he said, and I thought there was a tinge of relief in his voice. "I'm glad you've made that decision, Carrie. I think you'll be very happy at the ranch."

Happy? Was that the word, I wondered as we returned to the truck, aware that my panties were soaked once again.

More like frustrated, confused, humiliated and turned on, if today was anything to go by.

When we got back home, I took the bags of clothes up to the loft. I felt awkward about them, like they weren't really mine. I laid each item out on the bed and ran my hands over them. They were beautifully made—designed to be worn and loved for years. The dress came with a hanger, and I found a nail on the wall to hang it from. It sure looked out of place in this rustic room, and I wondered when I'd have a chance to wear it. I blushed at the sight of the underwear, reminded that Steele had seen it already, recalling the heat in his eyes when I'd picked out the lacy panties. A couple of pairs of pantyhose had appeared, too, size S.

I pulled off my old clothes and dressed in a new pair of jeans and a red plaid shirt, which was made from soft cotton, and fit nicely against my body.

I tried to pull my tight new boots on, but I couldn't do it by myself. I'd have to get Steele to help until they got worn in. The memory of him in the store, his arms wrapped around me, flashed into my mind again, with a rush of heat.

He was going to take care of me; punish me when I needed it.

But was that all?

A big part of me hoped not.

I took my boots and climbed back down the ladder.

But when I reached the ground floor, I startled.

Steele was waiting for me. Sitting on the hay bale again, his legs wide apart.

What have I done wrong now? Is he going to spank me again?

My body flooded with waves of anticipation and desire.

CHAPTER 6

Steele

I watched Carrie climb down the ladder, her small hands and feet negotiating the rungs. The sight of her petite curvy bottom swaying from side to side was sending my desire into overdrive.

I'd only meant to punish her this morning, but instead, I'd succeeded in giving myself the worst case of blue balls of my entire life. Not that I hadn't been aroused before. The way she'd pulled her jeans down so reluctantly... then that lovely rear in those pretty little panties bent over my lap... the way she'd squirmed and thrashed, trying to get away from me— *Sweet mother of God.* When I'd finished spanking her, her butt was as red as the blush on an apple, and I'd just about exploded in my pants.

Well, she and that butt of hers were mine now—

Mine to discipline.

Mine to punish.

And one day she'd be mine in all senses of the word.

When Carrie turned and caught sight of me sitting on the hay bale, her face filled with alarm. She thought I was going to spank her again. I didn't plan to, but with that sassy mouth of hers, a lot could change in a short time.

"Come here," I told her. "I'm going to show you how to polish your boots. It's the best way to soften them up."

Relief erased the tension in her features and she almost skipped over to me, swinging the boots in her hands.

I took a tin of polish and greased up a cloth real good, then picked up one of her boots and began to work it over. "Just like this," I directed, handing the items to her.

Carrie sat on the hay bale beside me and got to work. My chest filled with warmth. She looked beautiful like that—doing exactly what was required of her without complaint.

She did a good job, making sure every square inch was perfectly covered. When she'd finished with the first, she did the second one, too. I handed her a stiff shoe brush, and showed her how to buff the leather to a high shine. She worked with fierce concentration, forehead furrowed, elbows flying, and I understood she was trying hard to impress me.

When she was done, she looked up at me expectantly.

I took a deep breath, my heart beating faster than usual.

"My boots need cleaning, too," I said.

As soon as the words were out of my mouth, I knew I was crossing some kind of line.

Carrie scanned my filthy boots—which were still on my feet—and a look of distaste crossed her face. "Okay?" she said.

I stayed silent, letting her put the pieces together.

"You gonna take them off?" she muttered, her voice laced with reluctance.

"Nope." I crossed my arms, and stretched my legs out. "I

want you to polish them *in situ.*"

She screwed her nose up in that adorable way. "Really?"

"That's right, babygirl." Arousal deepened my voice. "I want you to get on your knees and polish my boots until they shine."

Her gaze dropped from my face to my boots. She didn't move.

"You disobeying me? After you promised to mind?" I half hoped she'd say yes; half-hoped I could find another excuse for pulling her pants down and seeing that lovely ass laid out over my knee. "This is part of our deal—you doing as you're told."

She was silent, no doubt turning over whether to refuse and give me some sass.

"Okay," she said at last.

Adrenaline raced through my body in hot, stirring loops. I handed her the brush I used to get the mud off, then I leaned back, feet wide apart, and indicated a spot on the floor in front of me.

Slowly, slowly, she kneeled on the wooden floor, in front of my right boot.

She began to scrub at the boot, gingerly at first, then, as the dirt came off, with more vigor.

The sight of her like that—on her knees, attending to me, the tip of her pink tongue showing between her lips—almost made my head explode. Desire built inside me, tightening my thighs, flooding to my cock. Before long, I was rock hard. The way I was sitting, there was no way of hiding it, and I figured there wasn't much point trying.

Instead, I kept taking deep, slow breaths as I watched Carrie carrying out my orders.

When she'd finished with one boot, she shuffled over and got to work on the other.

Finally, she put down the brush and looked up. Her gaze

fluttered to the bulge of my cock, unmissable beneath the fly of my jeans.

I held my breath, wondering how she was going to react.

She stumbled to her feet, her pretty green eyes wide and dazed. Beautiful and submissive. She'd gone into that deep submissive place that she'd learn to crave. I didn't dare shift my position. She looked as flighty as a wild pony, and I sensed that the slightest wrong move could send her bolting away from me.

She lifted her head and met my gaze and took a staggering step toward me, then another one, and the last threads of my willpower broke apart.

I wrapped my arms around her waist and pulled her to me. She lifted her chin up at the same moment, and I crushed my mouth against hers.

Her lips were soft. Small, but full, and tasting of raspberries. Nothing in my life had tasted as sweet. When I began to kiss her deeper, she gave a soft moan and opened for me, clinging to me, welcoming the intrusion of my tongue.

I held her tight, exploring her mouth, while her small body pressed against me, her breasts against my chest, one of her thighs rubbing up against my cock.

I was doing my best to hold back, but when her small hands lifted up and caressed my face, I was lost.

I reached for the press studs on her shirt and tore them apart. A moment later, her shirt was discarded on the hay bale and there she was, bared to my gaze. She was perfect—from her small, rounded shoulders, to the swell of her breasts in her innocent white bra, to the taut plane of her stomach.

Her eyes were big and stunned, but I sensed the hunger in her as well.

I grasped her hips, making her straddle my lap. The apex of her thighs brushed up against my swollen cock. *Jesus.* I was one step away from tearing off her jeans and taking her harder than I'd taken anyone before.

Then, to my amazement, she reached behind herself and, arching her back, she unhooked the fastener on her bra. I watched, mesmerized, as it slipped right off and her lovely breasts were bared to me. They were perfect, pert mounds, topped by dusky pink areolas, her perky little nipples pebbled with need.

I leaned forward and took one in my mouth. She gave a soft sigh of pleasure, and my cock surged, yearning to break free of my pants.

Like a man in a dream, I unbuttoned her jeans and she stood up and shuffled out of them.

I slipped my hand between her legs, and—holy hell—the outside of her panties was wet. Just like they'd been this morning when I spanked her ass. I pushed them aside and met soft fur and slick wetness. She groaned at my touch. I caressed her lightly, marveling at the feel of her. When her hand came down over mine, encouraging me to go inside, I slipped a fingertip inside her. She was soaked and I felt her clenching around me, but she was small—barely big enough for my finger.

I froze, yanked my hand away, and snapped back into reality.

"You're a virgin," I said.

She dropped her gaze away from me and nodded.

I took a shuddering breath and released her. "All right, babygirl. That's enough." I grabbed her shirt and held it up to her. "Put this back on."

"B-but I want to," she stammered.

I shook my head deliberately. "Doesn't matter. You're less than half my age. I'm not about to go busting your cherry."

Her face was full of confusion. "But, Steele—a lot of guys want that. If only you knew—" She broke off.

"Knew what?"

"Nothing." She passed a forearm across her forehead. Her cheeks were burning. "I'm ready, and I want my first time to be with you."

She slunk toward me again, her tender nipples inches from my face. Her small hand landed on my crotch. Dear God, if I wasn't about five seconds away from shooting my load.

Instead, I caught her hand. "I said no. Not now." Not when I was half gone with lust, ready to buck out of control. I'd hurt her.

"Let me at least take you in my mouth."

The thought of her on her knees, my cock tight between her cherry lips, appeared in a blinding flash behind my eyes.

But no. I was the one in control. She was drunk on a scene. I'd given her a little taste, and next time, she'd want more.

"Not today, babygirl." I rose to my feet. "You be good and do as I say. Put your clothes on, like I told you. You can stay out here for a while, take a moment for yourself. I'll tell you when you can come in and get dinner ready."

Leaving Carrie in the barn, I strode into the house. My cock was still rock hard. The only thing that would take the edge off right now would be taking myself in hand. But I wasn't going to give in to that. I'd already tested my control with that little taste of her submission. She was so young, so innocent. I kept forgetting that because she had so much sass and streetwise style. But she was new to all this, and I needed to remember that.

I had to keep my dark desires on a tighter leash.

I went to the tack room, grabbed Silver's bridle, and headed out to the fields. I'd go tend to the cows, and go on a long, long ride. Put a little distance between me and Carrie. It was the only way to keep her safe—from me.

CHAPTER 7

Carrie

I barely slept that night. I'd made sure to set the alarm on my phone, but I'd spent the night tossing and turning, and I was already awake when it went off.

It was still pitch dark outside, of course. I climbed down the ladder and washed up in the bathroom, shivering in the early-morning chill.

I was nervous about seeing Steele again. He'd been so cold with me last night when he got back from his ride. He'd cooked up dinner in silence, issuing curt instructions to me. Then he'd acted like he couldn't get his food down fast enough, before washing up and telling me he'd see me in the morning.

I was as confused as hell. He'd wanted me yesterday. The moment I'd gotten on my knees and looked up at him, I'd noticed that sexy bulge in his pants. And it had only gotten bigger while I'd worked on his boots. Then he'd taken me in his arms with such hunger, the raw need burning in his eyes.

I didn't get him. What kind of guy fingers a girl, then decides he can't have sex with her? Out of all my friends at high school, I was only one who was still a virgin, despite everything. Despite all the boys at school. Despite all the creepy guys my mom had brought home with her. I'd been waiting for the right one, and I'd decided that one was Steele.

But then he'd gotten all serious and moralistic. He'd acted like *I* was the one who'd started it, when he was the one who'd made me take my jeans down and lay my ass across his lap...

Well, screw him if he's going to be like this.

I checked the time on my phone again. I still had five minutes and twenty-six seconds before I was due to meet Steele at the door of the barn.

I decided I'd go greet the horses while I was waiting. I went to each of their stable doors, and called them by name. I'd learned their names yesterday—Misty, Moonshine, Calico, Violet, and Rex. Some of them ignored me, but Megan came to me, and blew her warm breath on my hand. She let me touch her nose, then I reached forward and patted the side of her neck. She seemed to like that, too, standing still for me, munching on her hay like it was gum. I loved her rich, fruity scent, the soft shine of her mane. I told her she was beautiful, and lucky that Steele was her owner, and her ears pricked up like she was listening to me.

I was so caught up in petting her that I didn't hear Steele approach until he was right behind me. I spun around guiltily.

"Sorry I wasn't by the barn door," I blurted out.

But he broke into a smile, his stern features transforming. My heart lifted. He looked sexier than ever this morning, in an indigo denim button-down that brought out the color of his eyes. My heart beat faster, and my stomach tingled.

He raised his hands. "That's fine. As long as you're up and about, I'm happy. And it looks like you and Megan are making friends. I was thinking you could start riding her today, maybe."

"Really?"

He nodded seriously. "Let's get to work first, though."

I followed him to the shed where the equipment was kept.

The task was the same as yesterday—take the horses out of the stall and muck them out. I knew the drill now, and I was getting quicker, Steele told me approvingly.

Yesterday's coldness seemed to have blown away on the wind. Had he just forgotten what had happened between us? It sure seemed like it. I glanced at him when he wasn't looking, trying to pick up on his body language. He seemed relaxed, and I didn't catch him looking at me once. Well, he seemed like a guy who made a decision and stuck to it. I just wished that my attraction to him hadn't quadrupled since he'd kissed me, stripped my clothes off, and sucked on my nipples—nipples that were now so hard, it hurt. I sighed. The only thing that would make them better would be his mouth on them again.

And that wasn't about to happen. I guess I should take his cue, and try to get over it.

* * *

Steele

CARRIE DID GOOD THIS MORNING: up on time, appropriately dressed in her new shirt and jeans, her hair neatly combed. I couldn't fault the way she mucked out the stables, either. She was trying to please me, and that cheered me up a little.

She wasn't anything like Victoria. My last submissive had pretended to like ranch life. She liked some of it—wearing four hundred dollar Frye boots she never let get too dirty. Petting the horses. Playing at a rancher's wife. She even submitted to my darker urges. We both tried to make it work. But in the end, it hadn't been enough.

My love hadn't been enough.

This was different, I told myself. Carrie was different. Unconsciously sexy, not manipulative like Victoria. Innocent —too innocent for me.

I hadn't slept well last night, tormented by the way I'd almost lost control. It wasn't Carrie's fault that she tempted my darkness. Hell, the last thing the girl was a flirt. But that had done nothing to kill my attraction for her. Whenever her back was turned, I couldn't help running my eyes over her body—her curvy little bottom sticking out so provocatively as she bent to shovel manure.

I'd promised she could stay for a while, but I'd better not lose control—of my heart, or the dangerous darkness that dwelt inside me.

Megan's stall was the last to be cleaned out. When Carrie had finished, she looked at me expectantly, awaiting my next instruction.

"I'll give you a lesson on Megan now, if you want?" I said.

Her eyes lit up. "Sure would," she said.

Leaving Megan tied to the fence, we went to the tack room, and I took a saddle and showed Carrie how to transport it over one shoulder.

I taught her how to lay it over Megan's back and tighten the girth, and how to persuade the horse to take the bit in its mouth. Megan tossed her head and complained a lot like she always did, but eventually Carrie managed to get the bit in her mouth and fasten the buckle behind her ears. Carrie was a quick study, I noticed. And she seemed to have a way with horses. Somehow, that wildness of hers seem to correspond to theirs.

I slung the saddle over Moonshine's back, and bridled him.

"All right, hop up, and we'll go into the corral," I told Carrie.

At that moment, I picked up the sound of a vehicle approaching down the track. I turned my head, expecting to see my brother, back from his trip early, but it was two Mounties—Dave and Trey, both good buddies of mine. They saluted a greeting.

"Police?" Carrie said.

"Yeah," I said carelessly, but when I glanced in her direction, I saw the color had drained from her face.

"Why are they here?" she hissed, her eyes huge.

"Guess they've come to—" I started to say. But before I could finish my sentence, she'd swung herself up into the saddle. She yanked hard on the rein—hauling Megan's head around—kicked her in the ribs, and she was off.

"What the—" I yelled.

But it was too late. Megan's hooves pounded across the yard and off into the open field.

"Something wrong?" Trey called.

"No—uh—I guess Megan's a little energetic this morning," I said, trying to keep my voice even.

"Want me to go after her?"

I glanced at his police-issue SUV. Whatever Carrie was up to, I sensed a car chasing her down would make things a whole lot worse.

"No, it's okay. I'll go find her. I'll catch you guys later." I waved casually, and kicked Moonshine into a trot.

The moment I was out of sight of the guys, I took off.

Carrie was already a dark spot in the distance. Where the hell did she think she was going? She wasn't an experienced rider yet. She might make a mistake, take a fall. And I wasn't there to catch her.

Cold sweat formed on my back as I pushed Moonshine into a gallop.

Megan was in full-on bolt mode, but Moonshine was a bigger, stronger horse, and we were soon on her tail. I prayed that Carrie wouldn't fall off. She was hunched forward again, clinging to Megan's neck, but by some feat of determination, she was managing to stay on.

I went out in a wide arc so I didn't scare her, then circled in, eventually drawing level.

"Pull on the reins," I yelled to her.

"I can't!" she screamed.

"I'm going to stop you now. Hold on." I brought Moonshine in front of Megan, and slowed him down to a trot, so Megan was forced to slow down, too.

In a few seconds, we'd halted. I leaped off Moonshine's back before he came to a complete stop. Quick as lightning, I went over to Carrie and grabbed her right off the horse. Her legs weren't strong enough to hold her up, and she crumpled.

"It's okay, babygirl. I've got you." She was trembling. I pulled her close, and she relaxed somewhat. Relief gave way to anger, and I took hold of her hips, and set her to face me. "What in God's name was that?"

"They've come for me, haven't they?" she whispered. She was panting, her eyes wild and panicked.

"Come for you? No." I shook my head. "Why would the police be after you?"

"What were they doing here, then?"

I shrugged. "They're buddies of mine. They come over often to shoot the breeze."

She stilled, then she took a deep breath, her small chest rising and falling convulsively. "It was a social call?"

"Yup. A social call, that's all. Now…" I shook her again. "You've got ten seconds to tell me why you think the police are on your tail. What are you mixed up in? Is it drugs?"

She stared up at me, and I gave her another little shake.

"Answer me."

"No." But she didn't explain. Her lower lip trembled, and a tear glided down her cheek. I couldn't take it anymore.

I caught her chin with my rough fingers. With my free thumb, I rubbed the wet mark away. "Tell me, babygirl."

"No." She wrenched her face away and wiped her arm across her tear-stained face. "I can't. I don't care what you do. You can kick me out right now, but I'm not telling." She folded her arms, and stared at me with a mixture of defiance and sadness.

I glared at her. My heart still thumped with adrenaline from having to chase her down. I had half a mind to spank it out of her right now. But this wasn't the place.

"Get back on the horse," I told her. Then I climbed back onto Moonshine's back, and took hold of Megan's bridle, so Carrie didn't get any ideas about bolting again.

We walked back to the ranch. I dropped Carrie off at the barn and told her to wait for me there.

The guys had gone already, as I'd anticipated. I untacked Megan and Moonshine and returned them to their stalls, then I walked some circles around the yard until I was calm enough to deal with my little felon.

* * *

WHEN I ENTERED THE BARN, Carrie was standing in front of the hay bale. Her face was pale, but her eyes were still burning with that wildness of hers.

75

Anger zipped through me like an electrical charge. I took a deep breath to get myself under control. The darkness inside me snapped its teeth like a beast, pacing in its cage. Now wasn't the time to let it out.

"I told you I couldn't abide liars," I said slowly; deliberately. "And now I find out you're in trouble with the police. I knew it. Knew there was a reason why you were so cagey and desperate for a job here. Tell me what you've done, right now."

"I can't tell you." She plonked her ass down on the hay bale and tried to yank the boots off. "I'll give you back all that stuff you gave me, and I'll just get my things and go." The boot held fast, and her face got redder and redder.

"Where are you going to go, Carrie?"

"Don't know." The first book clunked to the ground, and she went on to wrestle with the other one.

I stalked over to her. "No you don't, little one. I'm not letting you go so easily. Not until I know you're safe."

The second boot hit the ground. She blinked up at me, tears in her eyes. "Why do you care?"

"Because you're mine now. You gave yourself over to me. To protect. To discipline. But I can't protect you if you won't tell me the truth. You're going to tell me everything, right now."

A little tremor went through her, but she rolled her lips between her teeth and shook her head.

"All right. If that's how you want this to unfold." My hands went to the buckle of my belt. I unfastened it, and slid the entire belt loose from my jeans. "Last chance," I warned her.

She stared at the belt, eyes wide. "I can't."

"You're going to tell me, or I'm going to punish you, and then you'll tell me."

I brandished the belt between both hands, and a strange

calm took hold of me. I'd belted submissives before. Sure, we had been in a club and it was all a scene. But this wasn't play. This was real.

Carrie kept staring at the belt. If tensions weren't so high, I'd have said she looked mesmerized, almost intrigued. I'd punished her before and it had hurt, but also aroused her.

"Last chance," I repeated, and gentled my voice. "You can tell me, babygirl. You'll feel better when it's all out."

She shook her head, stubborn as ever. "I can't."

"Then you take your punishment."

Her chin came up. "Fine." She stood quietly and waited as I took hold of the hay bale and dragged it out from the side of the room.

"Take your jeans down," I told her, "and bend over the hay bale."

Carrie stood, looking from the hay bale to the belt in my hand and back again, as if she couldn't believe I was actually following through.

"Now," I said, my tone low and threatening.

She opened and closed her mouth one more time, then reluctantly, sulkily, she unbuttoned her jeans. She pulled them down to mid-thigh level, exposing a pair of cream lace panties.

"And the panties," I growled.

A little quaver cut through her bravado. "Do I have to?"

"Don't make me take them down myself. You won't like the consequences."

Her hands trembled as she hooked her fingers into the waistband. She hesitated, then yanked them all the way down.

I'd expected her to turn her back on me, but instead I was treated to the sight of her blonde pubic hair—a neat, tender triangle, her sex barely visible beneath. My cock surged again, and the memory of having my finger inside her yesterday exploded into my mind.

I indicated the hay bale with a tilt of my jaw. "Bend over it," I told her in a firm tone.

Her cheeks burned, but slowly, she turned around and began to hobble over to the bale. She clambered over it awkwardly, until her bottom was high in the air. Christ, the sight of those pale, round globes, presented so invitingly… She kept her slender thighs together but her pink lips were just visible beneath the peachy crack of her ass. It was all I could do not to take my cock out and plunge into her.

But I needed to break that stubbornness of hers—to show her I cared enough to discipline her when I said I would.

I kept the belt buckle in my hand and wrapped several loops around my fist, until two feet of cow hide remained. When I snapped it between my hands, she flinched.

I drew it back, and swung it against her ass.

Slap.

She gave a little gasp.

"I'm just getting started," I warned her.

I gave her six more—slap, slap, slap—until I'd covered her entire ass, barely raising any color from her skin. She made a little sound at each one—like a cat's mew, more in surprise than anything.

Adrenaline surged in my body, mingled with my anger.

"You don't go riding off without my permission," I told her. "You could've been hurt." I drew back my arm, and brought the belt down.

Crack.

She cried out. This time, a red stripe rose to the surface.

"You don't go lying to me."

Crack.

I brought the belt down on her right cheek this time.

She yelped.

"You don't run from the police."

Crack. Just below her left cheek.

"And you don't keep hiding things from me, even when you've been caught out."

Crack.

That one was a lot harder, and she yelled out for real. She kicked her legs up—as if that would protect her.

"Put your legs down and keep still," I instructed her. "Or it'll only get worse."

"Please, no more," she whimpered.

"Tell me what you're running from."

"I can't," she moaned, her voice choked with tears.

I looked at her ass, half red, half white now. "I've only given you four. I'm guessing it'll take another six or so before you're ready to give it up."

Crack.

"I'm gonna find out anyway."

Crack. Crack. One on each side. She yelled and wriggled, but stayed in position.

I laid my hand on her rosy flesh. It was burning hot. "Come on, babygirl. Whatever it is, it'll be better once you tell me."

She trembled under my touch. "Can't." She sniffled.

I took a step back, and she made a whimpering sound. But she still wouldn't give it up. She was as stubborn as a wild mare. But I knew how to tame her.

I raised my arm and gave her two in quick succession—

Crack. Crack.

Two sharp, stinging lashes that drew sharp cries from her.

"Please stop," she whimpered.

The belt whistled through the air. *Crack!*

It landed heavily.

"Please, sir," she yelped.

Crack!

"I'll tell you! I'll tell you everything."

I stilled. "You'll tell me?"

"Yes—just, no more, please."

She was properly crying now, in wet, sobbing gasps. Her body was spent, her thighs dropping apart, and I had a perfect view of her pussy, glistening with wetness.

I leaned forward and cupped it with a rough hand. She was drenched, soaked through, and she gave a wild, animal moan of need.

"You're wet, babygirl. So wet from this. So wet for me."

I drew back the belt and whipped her once more, all along her crack.

She yowled, but made no move to close her thighs.

"This was supposed to be punishment," I growled. I ran my finger up her cleft, spreading her juices up to her asshole—which was also exposed to my gaze—a perfect pink rosebud.

I grabbed my cock through my jeans. The urge to take her now was overwhelming. Take her hard. Possess every part of her. Make her mine forever.

She was so slippery, so ready for me, that my finger began to slide into her small hole almost by accident. Blood pounded in my head, in my cock, and I forgot about my anger, about how she'd lied to me, as my finger disappeared into her hot, tight asshole.

She clenched around me and let out a ragged moan.

"You like that?"

"Mhhhmm," she mumbled.

"You going to tell me the truth now?"

"Yes," she whispered.

"This is what you need, huh?"

"Uh huh."

I slipped a second finger into her tight pussy, and began

to finger her like that, sliding in and out of her two little holes.

It felt wrong, but so right. She kept her face buried in the crook of her arm, and whimpered and moaned and arched her back, begging me to go deeper.

I started to go harder and faster, my fingers rough and clumsy, but she took it all, wanting more and more. I reached forward and rubbed the tip of my pinkie across the little bud of her clit, and it wasn't long before she exploded. I felt her spasming all around my hand, tiny muscles gripping me while her whole body shuddered.

"Good girl," I murmured, rubbing her back while her orgasm died away.

When she finally lifted her head, her cheeks were tear-stained but her expression was a wonder to see—stunned and ashamed and satisfied, all at once.

She flipped around on the hay bale and sat her bare ass down.

Her gaze floated to the fly of my jeans, to my cock straining uncomfortably beneath the denim. When she reached for me, I didn't stop her. I looked down and watched as she unbuttoned my fly with inexperienced fingers, and my cock sprang out, massive and rock hard. She made a sound of surprise.

"You're going to suck my cock, and then you're going to tell me everything," I said.

Slowly, slowly, she moved her head toward it. I could tell she'd never done this before.

I held her head gently in my hands. "Open up," I told her, and brought it to her mouth.

The way her sweet lips parted for me was something I knew I'd never forget. I nudged at them with the head of my cock, and she stretched her jaw and tried to take me in.

I looked down at her, her panties still around her ankles, her sweet pussy exposed...

And I exploded.

I hadn't meant to do that. But it was too late. My hot seed spilled over her lips in pulsing waves.

She looked taken aback, but wiped her mouth discreetly.

I buttoned up fast and helped her to her feet, tugging her tight jeans back up.

"Now, we're going to go inside, have a hot drink, and you're going to tell me the whole story, okay?"

She nodded, seeming too stunned to do anything else.

CHAPTER 8

Carrie

I sat on the couch, hands wrapped around a
steaming mug of cocoa, waiting for Steele to come
out of his bedroom. My ass was throbbing, and it hurt to sit
down. But the pleasure of the orgasm he'd given me was still
tingling inside me in little after-shocks. It was the first time
another person had made me come, and it was on a whole
other level from the ones I'd managed for myself. I was so
glad Steele had been my first. That his rough-tender hand
had coaxed a climax out of me.

It meant nothing though; I knew that. When he found out
what I'd done, he'd kick me out. Hell, he'd probably hand me
over to the police himself. It was the kind of guy he was—
principled. It was one of the things I liked about him. Or I
would, in a different world, anyway.

Steele emerged from the bedroom. The angular bones of

his face seemed softer now—the fury of earlier gone out of him.

He was carrying a blue wool blanket, which he put over my lap and wrapped around me.

"Didn't think it was time to get the winter stuff out yet," he commented.

The blanket smelled clean and comforting. I snuggled under it, trying to enjoy this moment—the last second in my life where I would feel safe.

I felt sick at the thought of the change that I knew would come over him when he knew what I'd done. There would be no more cocoa and blankets and soft words. Just a prison cell and an orange jumpsuit.

He sat down next to me, his eyes narrowed with concern.

"Okay, tell me," he said.

I swallowed hard.

"I-I ..." I began. I took a deep breath, and started again. "My mom's boyfriend—"

I broke off again, hyperventilating. I couldn't get the words out. I clapped my hand over my mouth.

Steele took me by the shoulders gently. "He hurt you?"

"Yes—no—kinda." I closed my eyes, replaying that terrible scene.

When I opened them again, Steele's jaw was tight and his eyes were stormy.

"Tell me what he did, little one." His soft voice brought tears to my eyes.

I shook my head, trying to free my thoughts. "He was always real flirty with me. But recently, it got worse. He started to touch me, making out it was an accident, but I knew he meant to do it. Little comments here and there, like what a heartbreaker I was, and how I needed to watch myself. A few times, I woke up and caught him in my room. He was just standing over me. But I knew he was planning something. I started keeping a knife under my pillow—" I broke off again, tears springing to my eyes.

Steele took my hand and massaged my palm with his callused thumb. "Keep going."

"Then one night, he came into my room, and he didn't just look at me. He pulled back the covers. I made out I was still asleep. But when he sat down on the bed beside me and put his hand over my boob, I grabbed the knife and stabbed him. Right in the guts." I clapped my hand over my mouth to stifle my sobs. "I hated him so much," I choked out. "But I'm scared I killed him."

Steele put his arms around me, and pressed my head against his chest. "There, there," he murmured, rubbing my back in big circles.

I stiffened in surprise. Steele wasn't freaking out; he wasn't disgusted by me. He was being... *sympathetic?*

The shock of it released something inside me, something I'd been holding in tight all this time. My body shook all over as I broke into uncontrollable sobbing.

And Steele let me. He didn't tell me to stop crying. He just held me and let it happen.

I cried for a long time, and when I finally lifted my head, I was embarrassed to see that I'd soaked the front of his shirt with my tears. "Sorry," I muttered.

"Let me fix that." He eased away from me, went to the bathroom, and returned with a box of tissues. I was expecting him to hand them to me, but instead, he pulled one out and gently, gently dabbed my eyes and my drenched cheeks. Then he got a fresh one and held it over my nose.

"Blow," he said.

I did as he told me, and he wiped my snotty nose as tenderly as a loving father would do to a child. It felt nice. Weird, but nice.

"That's better," he murmured. He took me in his arms again and held me against his broad chest.

I rubbed my cheek on the soft fabric of his shirt, and a feeling of comfort went through me.

"And after that, you ran away? Tried to get as far away as you could?" he prompted.

"Yeah. I just knew I had to go north. I didn't think I'd be able to get to Canada, but I wanted to at least try. Then I met a sweet Swedish girl at a bus station in Utah. She told me about the Help Swap website, and gave me five bucks to use an Internet café. I found your ad—you know that part—and I decided I had to make it here.

"I hitched a couple of times, and then I managed to sneak inside a truck, somewhere near the border, and I hid. The driver found me on the other side, but I ran."

Steele drew back and scanned my face. "You were very brave," he told me.

I puffed my cheeks out. "But what if I killed my mom's boyfriend? I'll get the death penalty."

Steele's jaw twitched as he ground his teeth back and forth. "For your sake, I hope he's not dead. But I'd sure like to get my hands on him myself. What state was he in when you left him?"

"Bleeding and screaming on my bed," I said. "But I didn't hang around. I grabbed a bag, and ran."

"That piece of human garbage," Steele muttered. He looked like he was about to get up and punch the wall. "What side did you stab him on?"

I searched through my memory, recalling the way the knife had gone in easier than I'd expected. His scream. The blood welling up so fast—black and oozy in the darkness of my bedroom. My stomach turned over again. I'd already puked three times at the memory of the horror.

"I was facing him," I said, "so his left side."

"Good. Less chance you killed him on that side." Steele scratched at his stubble. "I need to think about what to do."

Terror clutched at me again. "You mean, you're thinking about turning me in?" I croaked.

He shook his head. "No. I'm not an advocate of vigilante justice, but you did what you had to."

"I know he would've raped me. I could tell from the way he grabbed me that he'd already made up his mind."

"I understand." He squeezed my shoulders.

I lifted my head to look him in the eye. "I'm so sorry I lied to you before. I'm not a liar, usually. I just had to protect myself. And I was so scared."

His eyes crinkled at the corners; shrewd but kind. "I know you were. I saw that in you right away. I could tell something bad had happened."

"So you believe me?" I asked, desperate for him to know I was telling the truth.

"I believe you, Carrie." He gave me a long, serious look, as if he was turning something over in his mind. "And I'm going to protect you."

"P-protect me, how?"

"Keep you safe here. From anyone who might come looking for you—if it comes to that."

I took a big breath. "Even the police?"

He was silent again. "Even the police," he said at last.

I stared at him, knowing it was a lot to ask.

"No one knows you're here, right?"

"Not a soul. I threw out my SIM right away."

"No one would expect you to have traveled north?"

I gave a little laugh. "I'm sure no one expects me to have made it out of Texas."

"What's this guy's name?"

I sighed. "Enzo Gutierrez. He's a loser. He thinks he's a gangster, but he just sponges off my mom."

"Any distinguishing features?"

I listed all the tattoos and scars I could think of.

Steele brought his lips to my forehead and planted a small kiss there. "Try not to worry, now, babygirl. I'm going to take care of everything."

"Everything?" I echoed.

He stroked my hair thoughtfully. "I'm going to keep you safe; give you everything you need. All the care and discipline you've missed out on."

That word again... I gave an involuntary shiver.

"And Enzo?" I mumbled.

"Let me look into it," he said in a tone I knew meant: *don't question me anymore.*

I trusted him. He was a grownup. Ex-military. A man who'd seen and done a lot in his life. He wasn't a wannabe gangster like Enzo. He didn't need to show off and try to look tough. His confidence came from his brains and maturity.

Steele began to stroke my cheek, and when his thumb chafed my lower lip, I tilted my chin toward him.

Suddenly, we were kissing again. It was more gentle than before, and I relaxed in his arms, relief radiating through me in waves.

He believed me. There was no way he would kiss me like that if he didn't.

I still couldn't believe this sexy, sophisticated guy was interested in me—a little girl from Nowheresville, Texas.

But it was happening.

Relief transformed into pleasure as his mouth possessed mine. Deeper and deeper he kissed me, his soft, firm lips drawing out my soul. Healing all my pain. All I could do was cling to him, dizzy and lightheaded.

When his tongue touched against mine, a fire lit inside me again. I willed him to undress me, to touch me all over.

But instead, he carried right on kissing me, holding me in his arms, all sweet and caring.

Eventually, we drew apart. We were both surprised that it had gotten dark.

"Stay right here. I'll be back soon," he told me. While he went to see to the animals, I stayed snuggled under the blanket, fizzy with relief and yearning.

Steele was going to take care of me. He wanted me. These two thoughts twined around my heart until it bloomed, like a rose breaking out from a patch of thorns.

I started to think about what had happened between us earlier that day.

All firsts for me. All scary and shameful and exciting by turns.

Steele pulling my panties down and whipping me. The shocking intrusion of his finger in my ass. The sight of his big, beautiful cock. Him coming in my mouth.

When Steele had forced me to bend over the hay bale and expose myself to him, I'd almost wet myself in embarrassment. But then I'd heard the catch in his breath as he saw my private parts for the first time. A weird, squirmy bolt of arousal had gone right through me. The thrashing with the belt hurt like crazy but it was offset by the ache in my pussy, the knowledge of his desire for me.

I'd been shocked when he slipped his finger inside me, probing my most private place like he owned it. I wondered if he'd do it again. If he'd try to do more than that.

Surely his cock was too massive for that. Too massive for my mouth, even. I'd freaked out a little at the sight of it, knowing there was no way I'd be able to suck it good. I had no idea what I was doing when I put my lips on him. I was glad he was my first, though, and that I hadn't sucked off some stupid boys behind the bleachers at school.

I loved the sound he made when he came, the way he exploded on my tongue, all hot and salty.

I wanted to please him so bad. To show him I wasn't some inexperienced little girl.

Even though I was.

* * *

WHEN STEELE CAME BACK, he made us some food—beef stew with potatoes.

"Just this time, you can eat on your lap," he told me, with a kind look.

When he'd taken the empty plates away, he held me in his arms again and we kissed some more. But, before long, my eyelids started to droop. He scooped me up and carried me up to the barn. With my arms wrapped around his neck and legs dangling either side of him, I felt like a little girl. I rested my head on his shoulder and let it happen. Let that drowsy, secure feeling suffuse my body.

The chill of the outdoors woke me up a little, but when Steele carried me up the ladder, then deposited me in the warm bed, I soon got sleepy again. More than anything, I yearned for him to stay with me, to hold me in his big arms all night. But he kissed me on the cheek and left me alone.

The last thought that crossed my mind before I fell asleep was: *I've never felt so safe.*

CHAPTER 9

Steele

$\mathcal{M}$y chest ached for everything Carrie had been through. The things she'd told me knocked me sideways. Who did that to a girl? A girl asleep in her bed?

After I'd put Carrie to bed, I paced around the house like a caged animal. The thought of that piece of crap touching her turned my blood to molten lava. He'd treated her like a piece of meat that was his for the taking. Thrown her in the worst kind of catch twenty-two situation—having to choose between getting raped, or potentially killing her attacker. I didn't blame her for stabbing him. I had half a mind to track him down and stab him myself.

It had taken her a lot to confess to me. The fear in her eyes as she'd told me had cut me to the quick. She was a good girl; a brave one. Now I understood her wildness, her flightiness a whole lot better. She'd had no one to protect her. She'd been alone all this time—all her life, really, by the sound of it.

Well, I was going to look after her now. Do whatever it took to protect her, to make sure she never had to go through anything like that again. I made that vow to myself then and there.

I sat up late on the computer, scouring the Internet. I used an IP blocker and went through all the news sites, searching her abuser's name. But there was nothing. I searched the local news sites in Texas; I even went on the FBI's wanted list. It was all a blank.

The longer I searched and came up with nothing, the more relief I felt. I was no expert on violent crime, but surely if someone had been stabbed to death, there would be some record of it. Hopefully, he'd made it to a hospital and gotten patched up. Probably blamed it on gang warfare.

I'd keep on checking the news every day, I decided. Reassure myself that no one was looking for Carrie. And in the meantime, I'd keep her safe here at the ranch. She deserved that. I was going to give her the care and security she so desperately needed.

I was glad I'd given her some comfort today, eased away the tension in her shoulders, the terror from her eyes. When she'd finished confessing, she'd looked a lot calmer, like I'd shifted the burden away from her.

I hadn't meant to start kissing her again, but she was so soft in my arms, and that honeyed scent of hers was irresistible. I longed to take her to my bed, to sleep with her in my arms all night long. But she needed care tonight—and routine. There would be time for everything else later. I knew that as sure as an instinct. Just like one of my horses, I had to get her disciplined first, or I'd only encourage her in her wild ways.

I only hoped, with a little control and a lot of care, she would turn out good.

And then she'd never feel the urge to run away again.

* * *

NEXT MORNING—BEFORE I'd even gotten out of bed—Carrie was instantly on my mind.

What if she's changed her mind during the night? Gotten spooked and left already?

The thought brought an unwelcome jolt of adrenaline to my veins.

But when I threw my clothes on and walked outside, she was already at the stables, hanging over Megan's door, talking to her. I couldn't hear what she was saying, but Megan was paying attention, her little gray ears pricked up curiously.

I strode over to Carrie.

Then I stopped. After the way we'd been yesterday, I didn't know how to greet her.

But when she turned around at the sound of my approach, her face lit up with delight. She rushed over to me and threw her arms around my waist.

My heart lifted so fast, it just about shot out of my mouth. I pushed my face into her tangled but clean hair, and inhaled her scent. For no reason at all, I was laughing a little.

"How did you sleep?" I asked.

"So well. I feel like a new person. Thank you for everything, Steele." When she tipped her head back to meet my gaze, her eyes were bright and clear, and I knew everything had happened for the good yesterday.

"You're very welcome," I replied. I scanned her pretty, impish face—taking in her snub nose, freckles, and that pursed, ripe cherry of a mouth, and desire stirred in me. Her lips parted expectantly, and I was sorely tempted to dip my head and capture them in a kiss.

But I didn't.

She was mine. I felt it deep in my bones. But we weren't

boyfriend and girlfriend. Nor was she my submissive. Not yet, anyway. She was so innocent, she probably didn't know what BDSM was.

Now wasn't the time to teach her.

I shoved my hands in my pockets, and told her I'd searched the Internet and there was nothing relating to her abuser so far.

She gave a deep sigh of relief. "That's so good to hear."

I drew away from her, and clapped my hands together. "Okay, go brush your hair, then let's get to work."

She pouted a little, until I gave her a stern look, then she ran off to the bathroom.

* * *

THE SUN CAME UP bright and clear; and my mood expanded with it. It was a beautiful, crisp fall day, and I had Carrie to take care of. I'd never dated a woman so much younger than me; never really thought of it. But this thing between us felt right. Natural. What my subconscious had been seeking all along: a girl who had a desperate need for protection and discipline.

I'd kind of assumed I was destined for a life of loneliness out here on the ranch. After Victoria, I never thought I'd find a woman who'd want to live out here with me. But was it possible Carrie could be that woman? From a place deep in my soul, I yearned for that to be the case.

She came back from the bathroom, hair neatly brushed, hands thrown out to the sides clownishly. "Ta-dah!" she shouted.

I couldn't help smiling at her antics. Underneath that hard shell and bluster, there was a sweet girl. I was going to protect that innocent core of her. At the same time, I'd show her the darker side of desire. It would be a fine line, but I could walk it. And I had a feeling I was going to enjoy that process very much.

* * *

"WHAT'S NEXT, BOSS?" Carrie asked once she'd wheeled the manure out to the heap at the back. She wiped her hands on the back of her pants, and grinned at me with a combination of eagerness and mischief.

"Well, I thought you could groom Megan today," I said.

"Can I ride her after?"

I snorted. "After that stunt you pulled yesterday? No chance."

Fury flashed in her eyes. "You know why I did that yesterday. It was a one-off, and it won't happen again."

I shook my head. Two spankings, and all that feistiness was still there. It hadn't gone down a single notch. Just like a wild pony. They could turn docile one minute, but the next day they'd be as wild as ever, as if they'd forgotten everything you'd taught them.

"You could have hurt Megan," I said sternly. "You don't go racing off a horse like that without knowing the ground. She could have fallen down a gopher hole or something. If she'd broken a leg, I would've had to shoot her in the head, and that would have been on you."

She gasped. "Shoot her?"

"Yup, there's no fixing a horse's legs when they're broken."

Carrie went to Megan and pressed her forehead against Megan's nose. "I'm so sorry," she muttered, stroking the horse's neck. "I was just real scared and not thinking straight."

"And this is exactly what we're going to work on— thinking straight. Which begins with routine and discipline. Now, I'll let you brush Megan." I handed her a currycomb. "Don't be afraid to put some elbow grease into it."

Carrie was hesitant at first. But I put my hand over hers on the brush and showed her she didn't need to be too gentle. When she could see that Megan was enjoying it, she relaxed and got into her task. Forehead furrowed, lips pressed together, her face was a charming picture of concentration. I could tell she wasn't thinking, wasn't worrying or remembering. She was here, in the moment, and it was beautiful to see.

She wasn't used to paying attention to detail though, and I pointed out a few spots she'd missed on Megan's thick coat. She was nervous about brushing Megan's legs—with good reason, because Megan had been a real kicker when I first got her. But I showed Carrie how to do it—how to let Megan know she was coming, so she didn't startle and kick out.

When Carrie had finished the rear legs, I handed her a nylon brush and she brushed Megan's mane and tail until they were silky.

She stood back and admired her handiwork.

"Looks like a show pony doesn't she?" I said.

"She sure does." Her eyes sparkled with pride. "I'll make sure she looks like that every day."

I nodded, pleased. "I know you will."

When I led Megan back into the stable, Carrie's face fell. She'd apparently expected I'd relent in the end.

Well, she needed to learn that I always stuck to my guns. No point making rules if you broke them all the time.

"What's next?" she demanded in a slightly sulky tone.

"You can watch me lunge Rex for a while," I told her.

I went to his stable and started the process of getting a collar on his head. I'd bought him at an auction a month earlier. He was a wild horse that someone had tried to break, and screwed up in the process. He was kind of my special project. I didn't really expect him ever to be rideable. But if I could civilize him a little, then I'd see it as a success.

Rex fought and kicked, ears back, eyes rolling, showing the whites. But eventually I got his head collar on, and led him out of the stall. Well, it was more like battling than leading. It took all my strength to stop him from bolting. I told Carrie to go and stand on the far side of the corral fence, and I dragged Rex in on the lunge rain. Inside the enclosure, he reared and bucked and did just about anything he could to fight me. But I kept pulling him along, using a lunge whip to keep him at a distance. Eventually, he kind of settled—figured out what I wanted from him, and consented to run around approximately in the circle, eyes rolling the whole time, and foam flying from his lips.

I kept at it for a good twenty minutes, until he'd tired himself out.

"He's sweating a lot," Carrie said from behind me when I brought Rex back to the stable. I'd been so focused on making sure that Rex didn't kick me in the head that I'd lost track of where she was.

"It's all fear," I told her. "If it was one of the other horses, I'd brush him off now. But there's no way in hell he'd tolerate that."

Now he was calmer, and he munched on his feed happily. Carrie hung over the stable door and watched him.

"It was amazing the way you controlled him," she commented. "I could see how wild he was, but by the end, he respected you."

I snorted. "I'm not sure Rex respects anything. He was a fighter—you can tell by all the scars on his body. A dominant stallion. Horses like him weigh almost ten times as much as a man, but you've got to show them who's boss. Show them you're worth submitting to."

Carrie turned to look at me, and there was something

questioning, curious, in her gaze. And as I thought about the wildness of the horse and the wildness of the small, feisty girl in front of me, an idea began to form in my mind.

A dark, exciting idea.

"Come on," I said. "We're going to the barn."

She startled, trepidation flashing across her features. "What for?"

"We're going to do some training of our own," I said over my shoulder as I strode ahead.

Carrie began to follow me but at a distance, her steps sluggish.

"Come on, girl, keep up," I called.

Once we were inside the barn, I switched on the overhead light, and the bare bulb filled the room with a yellowish glow.

I looked around, at the wooden uprights and horizontal beams, some with hooks attached, for hanging various things from. I hadn't worked out all the details of what I had planned, but I was surrounded with infinite possibility—all it took was a little imagination and a girl who was in need of a firm hand.

"Sit down over there." I pointed at the hay bale which was where I'd left it after I whipped her yesterday. "I'll be back in a minute."

I went to the tack room and returned with an array of leather equipment.

Carrie was sitting with her legs crossed. She looked bratty and defiant, but she was also fidgeting nervously. I smiled to myself. She reminded me of one of my horses when it was acting up.

I dumped all the stuff on the bale beside her.

"Now," I said. "It's come to my notice that your posture is terrible—like a lot of young people—and you can't expect to have a good seat on a horse if you can't hold yourself up straight."

Carrie shrugged.

"Do you agree?"

"Guess so."

"Stand up and take a turn about the room. I want to see if you can fix it by yourself."

"You serious?" Her expression turned sassy, teenagery. She was one beat away from rolling her eyes at me.

Irritation flared in me and I worked my jaw back and forth. "Yes, I'm serious. Is there a problem?"

"Seems kind of dumb."

I clenched my fists. "You sassing me again, little one?"

She rolled her lips between her teeth but then answered. "No, Steele."

"Good girl. This is part of your training. And when I tell you to do something, you do it. Unless you want another taste of the belt." I raised a brow, and she flushed. I chuckled to myself. I'd have to be careful. Belting her wasn't a total punishment.

Dragging her feet a little, she began to trail around the room, approximately in a circle. She kept looking back at me as if she couldn't quite believe what I was making her do. Her shoulders were rounded; her arms hung at her sides.

"You want me to use the lunge rein on you?" I called.

"What?" She frowned.

"Want me to treat you like a wild horse?"

"No. 'Course not."

"Well, straighten up then."

She tried, but I didn't see a whole lot of difference.

Shaking my head, I walked out of the barn and went into the house.

I returned with a book, which I held out to her. "This is our family Bible. Me and my brother aren't real observant these days, but it's been in the family for generations." I opened the cover and showed her the flyleaf, upon which the whole family tree had been written. One name after another in faded cursive script. I was proud of it, touched to see those generations of dedication.

"I'd hate to see something happen to it," I told her. "So when you put it on your head and walk around, you're going to make sure it stays there. Understood?"

I handed her the Bible. She frowned at it uncomprehendingly.

"Have you done this before?"

"No," she mumbled.

I shook my head. As a child, my grandma had made me and my brother and all our cousins take turns around the house with the Bible on our heads—to teach us to face life with a straight back. The sort of discipline Carrie needed.

"Go on. Balance it on your head and start walking."

Hesitantly, Carrie put the Bible on her head, fumbling it around until it stayed there by itself. Then she began to walk at a shuffling pace, hands held out in front of her and eyes full of trepidation. It was kind of comical to see.

But she hadn't gone ten steps when the book fell off her head, and she barely caught it in her hands.

"Try again," I told her. "This time, don't shuffle. Lengthen your stride. I want you to walk confidently."

"How can I lengthen my stride?" she exclaimed, full of indignation. "It makes my head bounce about too much!"

"Exactly. When your posture is good, your head doesn't bounce."

She tried again, and again, but her personal best was twelve paces before the book dropped off.

I sat down on the hay bale and watched her, the idea I'd been turning over flaring in my veins like electricity.

She came to a stop in front of me. "Can't do it," she said sulkily.

"You can. And you will," I said.

"This is stupid." She slapped her hand against her thigh.

"Girls half your age can manage this."

"Guess I left it too late to learn."

"It's never too late. But if you want to learn something, you've got to put the effort in. You can't just give up when things seem hard."

That was what was wrong with her generation. Technology made everything easy. Kids felt like they didn't need to try anymore. Well, I was going to make sure she turned out right.

I looked her up and down. What she needed was to feel vulnerable. More vulnerable than she'd ever felt before. It was the only way to tame her to my will.

"I want you to try again," I told her. "But this time, undressed."

She blinked. "Undressed?"

"You heard me." With an effort, I kept my eyes on her face, and set my jaw.

"But why?"

"Because you behave a lot better when you're naked."

She continued to stand in front of me, arms crossed, not moving.

"You need this discipline, babygirl. I'm going to give it to you. Do well, and you'll get a reward."

She looked intrigued at that but didn't move.

I raised my hand and snapped my fingers in front of her face, just as I would with a sub.

She jolted to life. With hurried fingers, she unbuttoned her shirt and discarded it, followed by her boots and jeans, until she was standing in front of me in just a pink bra and panties. Heat flooded my cock and I hardened instantly. I leaned forward so it wasn't so obvious.

"And the rest. No need to be shy. I've already seen all there is to see."

Her face went beet red. But she reached behind her back for her bra clasp.

Good. She knew better than to disobey me.

I stopped breathing as her pert, round breasts were revealed to me again. It wasn't cold in the barn, but her nipples were erect, two hard little buds. Then, more slowly, she eased down her panties, covering herself with her hand at the same time.

I suppressed a smile. She was about to find out that wasn't going to fly with me.

I returned the Bible to her. "Put it back on your head, and try again."

She soon discovered that she couldn't hide her sweet pussy from me *and* make sure she didn't drop the Bible, and her hands rose up in front of her again.

This time, her posture was different. Ramrod straight. And what an effect it had. Her shoulders went back, lifting her little breasts higher, so her erect nipples pointed toward the ceiling and her round, pert rear was displayed at a lovely angle.

She started off at a shuffle again. But little by little, she figured out that she could take bigger steps. Her hands dropped to her sides, and she began to walk more confidently.

I watched her, my erection raging beneath the zipper of my jeans. This was what she needed, I told myself. But it was all I could do not to grab her and ravish her over the hay bale.

When she'd completed a full turn, I gave her more

instructions—shoulders back, hands on hips, take bigger strides—and she did as she was told.

She completed three full turns to my satisfaction, and I instructed her to stop. She stood in front of me uncertainly, but didn't try to hide her body with her hands any longer. Instead, she awaited my next instruction, hands on her hips, and nipples harder than ever.

When I allowed my gaze to drop, I saw that her sex was glistening beneath the thatch of pale golden fur. I took a ragged breath. She was aroused. Maybe as aroused as I was. She was so ripe, so ready to be claimed.

Her cheeks were flushed, her eyes dark, pupils dilated. I saw how much she wanted to submit, to please me.

I made her wait as I turned over several ideas in my mind, letting her apprehension grow.

I thought about tying her up, spreading her wide against the wall.

Yes, that would come later.

But today, I wanted her to think of herself as a wild pony that needed to be tamed. To really feel it, deep in her bones.

I grabbed a few rough blankets I kept in the barn, and laid them in a big square on the floor. It would pad her knees a little, but not much.

"I want you to take one turn around the room on your hands and knees," I told her.

She frowned. "Crawl? Like an animal?"

"Not like an animal—like a girl who's doing my bidding."

While she continued to glower at me with a mixture of defiance and confusion, I retrieved an object from the hay bale.

My favorite riding crop. All black, Italian leather, from its handle to the keeper on the tip.

I tapped it lightly against my thigh. She stared at it, as if hypnotized.

"On your knees," I said. My voice sounded rough in my ears, practically a growl, and it had an electrifying effect on her. She went down on all fours on one of the blankets.

"The faster you carry out my orders, the faster you can stand up again."

I ran the leather keeper all the way along her back, from the nape of her neck to the crack of her ass. She twitched and flinched like a nervous horse. I pressed down harder on the back of her neck.

"Now, drop your head, and arch your back."

With a grunt of discomfort, she did as she was told, making a beautiful curve in her spine.

I went behind her and tapped the soft flesh of her inner thighs. "Part your legs a little."

She followed my order.

Jesus, the sight of her, all exposed to me, like an offering. Her wet pink pussy, her little bud of an asshole. All sweet and perfect. I swung the crop back a tad and gave her a tap on her pussy lips.

She gasped.

"Like that?"

"Mhhmm," she mumbled.

I followed it up with two more, then laid the rod against her cleft, so it pressed up against all her sensitive areas. She made a sound of need, and I drew it back and forth, creating a little friction. When she pushed back on it with a sigh, my cock twitched yet again. She was a naughty, hungry girl. And I'd give her what she needed. But first she had to earn it.

"You're going to remain in this position," I told her. "Every time I tell you to crawl. Back arched, bottom up, thighs apart. Do I make myself clear?"

"Uh huh," she muttered.

I swatted her ass, harder this time. The crop slapped against her bare skin and she yelped.

"I said, do I make myself clear?"

"Yes," she said, more loudly.

"Yes, Sir!" I barked.

"Y-yes… *Sir*?" she muttered, her voice full of questions.

I swatted her again and again, and each time, she yelped, more in surprise than pain. "When you answer a question, you call me Sir, okay?"

"Sir. Yes, Sir," she shouted out.

"Okay, good." A wave of satisfaction went through me, along with a fresh burst of arousal. "Now, move."

Reluctantly, she began to crawl across the floor, and I followed her, using my crop all the way. Soon, her behind was crisscrossed with pretty pink stripes. Now it was warmed up, I began to work it harder, alternating my strokes from side to side; across the middle of her cheeks; at the tops of her thighs, now and then a quick sting on her exposed pussy. When she went too fast, I held her back, making her take her time; maintain her beautiful posture.

When we'd completed two laps, I decided we were done. I sat down on the hay bale, legs wide apart, cock jutting up like a totem pole. There was no point trying to hide it.

"Come here," I told her.

With a grateful look, she pushed up onto her feet and came to me. I saw her knees were red and sore-looking. She wasn't going to forget this lesson in a hurry, I was certain.

Without me saying anything, she laid herself across my lap, bottom up, her torso and legs resting on the hay bale. A lovely, pleasing sight.

I examined her hot flesh. Deep pink stripes covered both her cheeks, from top to bottom, but the skin wasn't broken anywhere. The marks would be mostly gone by tomorrow, I concluded. When I laid my hand flat on her left cheek, Carrie shuddered.

"What is it?" I muttered.

"Feels good," she said in a tight voice.

"You want more?"

"Mmmhm," she groaned.

I stilled. Was she really saying what I thought she was saying? My pulse sped up.

"You want me to spank you again?"

"Uh-huh."

"Then ask me."

"I need to be spanked, Sir."

Blood boiled in my veins. My wild girl wanted me to punish her now? My head just about exploded, along with my cock.

I brought my hand down hard on her ass, and she cried out. Her skin was primed now and I didn't need to be gentle.

I sighed. Those red stripes were so pretty, but no substitute for my hand connecting with her flesh. That satisfying *slap!* sound. I spanked her again and again, her cries and squirming driving my desire.

She was crying out words now, mainly nonsense, until one phrase disentangled itself from the rest:

"Please, Daddy!" she yelled.

I froze, my hand still poised high in the air.

"What did you say?" I demanded.

She stiffened, and a silence rang out between us.

CHAPTER 10

Carrie

$\mathcal{M}$y cheeks burned. What the hell had I just said?

"I-I don't know," I stammered.

I'd been so caught up in the moment. So given over to the twin flames of pain and arousal consuming my body that I had no idea what had been coming out of my mouth.

"You called me Daddy," Steele said.

Heat flooded my face. "No."

"You did," he insisted.

"Why would I—" I began.

But I knew the answer to my own question. As crazy as it seemed, I did think of Steele as a daddy. Not like my daddy—because I'd never known my real father. And not like the endless stream of dudes my mom had tried—in vain—to get me to call Daddy. But something else. Something I didn't

107

have the words to explain—an older guy who was taking care of me and disciplining me when I needed it.

Is that a daddy?

"Come here." Steele lifted me off his lap, flipped me over, and took me in his arms.

And, unexpectedly, I burst into tears.

"Oh, honey," he murmured. "Everything's okay. It's all okay—whatever you're feeling."

I pressed my face into the crook of his neck and he rocked me. He actually *rocked me.* And it soothed me in a deep, primal way.

He waited patiently until I was all cried out.

"Shit, I keep crying on you," I mumbled, wiping my eyes.

"Did you mean to call me Daddy?" he asked me gently.

"No—I'm sorry. I know it was weird." I dipped my head, hiding my face.

"Carrie…" He hooked his thumb under my chin and lifted it until I was forced to look at him.

His eyes were vivid blue, and questioning. "It wasn't weird. None of your feelings are weird. I just want to understand."

I sighed. "You call me babygirl a lot. I thought… I guess I got confused. I mean, my subconscious did, or something."

His forehead furrowed thoughtfully, as if he was searching for the right words. "What I'm really asking is whether that idea appeals to you?"

I blinked rapidly. "Y-you mean… you mean…" The words were on the tip of my tongue, but I couldn't voice them.

"Of me being your daddy," Steele supplied.

My stomach turned over. It was a scary but excited feeling. Kind of like when you're at the top of a rollercoaster and it's just beginning its downward plunge.

"D-does it appeal to *you?*" I asked.

He didn't answer immediately, then he gave one of his

serious, deep nods. "I do. I like it a lot, Carrie. But only if you're equally invested in it. I don't want to force you into anything."

"I like it, too," I said in a small voice. "I mean... I'm invested."

He laughed, then I laughed, too, and it broke the tension between us.

I could tell he was being careful not to push me; really making sure I was into it. And I liked that a lot. I knew it meant he cared for me. He wasn't going to force me into something I didn't want.

I shook my head. "No, I've decided."

Such a look of relief crossed his face that my heart twinged. "I'm so glad to hear that, baby. I'm going to be a very good daddy to you."

I smiled at him and warmth filled my body. No one had taken care of me before. I'd pretty much raised myself. The thought of this was... amazing and overwhelming.

"How much do you know about BDSM?" Steele asked, stroking my hair.

I wrinkled my nose. I knew kink existed—I'd heard muffled sounds coming from porn my mom's boyfriends watched sometimes. But I tried not to think too much about that.

"Uh, I know some people like to be spanked. Tied up. Humiliated. Stuff like that."

"That's not all there is to BDSM, babygirl. There are many different types of relationships and kinks."

"Fifty Shades of Grey?" I asked, and his nostrils flared in the way they sometimes did when he was annoyed.

"More like colors of the rainbow. Many different shades." He fisted a handful of my hair and gently tipped my head back. "I can be your daddy. You can be my babygirl. I'll love you and protect you and discipline you when you need it."

For some reason this made me blink back tears. "Why me? I'm nobody special."

His blue eyes turned stormy. "That's where you're wrong. And I'm going to discipline and love you until you understand that." He released my hair and smoothed it away from my face. "We should set some ground rules."

"Like what?" This was all so new to me, I couldn't imagine what these rules might relate to.

"Discuss what's okay and what's not. Like a safeword—if you don't like something I'm doing."

"Safeword?" I echoed.

He took a deep breath, his big chest rising and falling. "When you shouted out before—did you really want me to stop?"

I shook my head slowly, thinking. "No, I don't think so. I was caught up in the moment. But I wasn't at my limit or anything."

This seemed to please him a lot. "And that's why safewords are important, baby. Sometimes, during play, you might shout out things in the heat of the moment—like *stop* —that you don't really mean. So it's good to have an unrelated word. And if you ever say that word, everything stops immediately."

Steele sure knew a lot about this kind of stuff. I'd been wondering if he'd done anything like this before, and here was my answer. I loved that he was so experienced, that he knew so much.

He continued playing with my hair. "Some people use red, orange, etc. It could be anything."

I thought about all the times in my life I hadn't felt safe.

"Strawberry," I said. "That's my word."

"Okay." He traced a line from my jaw to my lips. "Strawberry it is. And I hope you never have to use it. Because that would mean I hadn't understood all your needs, like a daddy should. But if you ever feel like something's too much, don't ever hesitate to shout it out, okay?"

I nodded, but my stomach was a little jumpy as I wondered what *too much* could mean.

"I'll spank you often. Most days. At least in the beginning."

I stuck out my lower lip, and he chuckled.

"Trust me, babygirl. Daddy knows what's best for you."

I opened my mouth to tell him that I didn't need my ass spanking all the time. But I stopped. Because I'd just asked him to do it to me. I didn't know why at the time. All I knew was I yearned for that dark, arousing sensation of his hand coming down on my ass.

And when he spanked me, I felt better. Like all the things that were mixed up in my head unraveled. All the times I'd been told I was bad, that I wasn't worth anything, were flattened and smoothed away like beaten steel. Transformed from something rough and ugly, into something good and strong.

"I'm going to take you inside and give you a rub down," he said, breaking through my thoughts. He got up, sweeping me up into his arms, and carried me out of the barn, not seeming to care that my clothes were left behind. The cold air hit my bare skin and I shivered. But soon we were back in the cozy warmth of the ranch house.

He deposited me on the couch and wrapped the blanket around me again. "I'll fix us something quick to eat," he said.

Minutes later, we were sitting side by side, eating cheese melts. It was the second time in a row that Steele had broken his rule of only eating at the table, but I decided not to mention it, in case it got him riled up.

When we were done, he stacked the plates in the dishwasher and then led me to the bedroom.

"Slip under the comforter," he told me.

"Really?" I blurted out before I could stop myself. This was his private place. I didn't feel like I was entitled to share it with him.

He grinned and flung back the coverlet. "Of course. Get in."

I was still a little cold, and I snuggled under the soft, blue fabric. His pillow smelled of fresh laundry, along with his spicy, outdoorsy scent.

He turned up the heater. I tried not to stare too blatantly as he stripped off his jeans, followed by his shirt, until he was wearing nothing but a pair of black stretchy shorts. He was semi-hard, and the sight of his erection made my pussy burn with need.

He was all perfect, sculpted muscle. Every bit of him was in shape—from his shoulders, to his chest, to the sexy contours of his abs. His thighs were thick like tree trunks, and his biceps were huge and bulky. After the way I'd seen him wrestling Rex under control, I didn't need to question where all that muscle came from. No one I knew from home had a body like that. It didn't come from the gym, but from hard, outdoor work, and it was as sexy as hell.

"Have you warmed up?" he asked, and I saw a new softness in his eyes.

"Yup. Plenty," I told him.

"Then flip over, and I'll rub you down."

I turned onto my front and he began.

His hands were firm, soothing, as he worked over my shoulders and my back, easing out the knots and tension.

"That's so nice," I murmured.

"Just relax," he muttered, his voice low and raspy. "This is all about making you feel good."

I felt great—never better. I pressed my face into his pillow, inhaling his sexy scent, breath after breath, while his fingers caressed me.

He skated over my ass with a light touch, no doubt figuring it couldn't take much pressure, then he worked on my legs. When he reached my thighs, he eased them apart a little, and just like that I was wet again; aching for him.

His hands moved higher and higher, and I bit down on my tongue to stop myself from making a sound. I wasn't sure if this was supposed to be sexy or just relaxing, but when I heard his breathing getting heavier, I knew he'd picked up on my arousal.

He eased my thighs further apart and I could tell he was looking at me again, taking me in. When he spread my ass cheeks, I squirmed. It was embarrassing having him see my most private place like that, and I was glad my face was hidden.

Suddenly, he trailed a fingertip along my slit, up to my ass. When it touched my small hole, it was wet with my juices. I held my breath as he circled it, scared he was going to finger my ass again.

Hoping that he would.

"Turn over," he said instead.

When I flipped onto my back, I saw his eyes were full of fire, his cock straining against the fabric of his shorts. He leaned over me and began to massage my breasts in soft, circular motions, until my nipples got so hard, they hurt. Then he stroked my stomach, my hips, and my thighs, before easing my legs apart. I tensed automatically.

"Don't fight me, little one," he said. "I want to see you."

I forced my thighs to go slack so he could spread me as much as he wanted.

"So pretty," he murmured, and I squirmed again. This felt vulnerable too, in a different way from when I was lying on my front.

When he began to caress my outer lips, my whole body jolted. Then he parted them, and peered at me.

He examined me like a doctor—well, like a very pervy doctor—while I fidgeted and my cheeks burned hot.

His fingertip probed a little at my entrance. "You really are a virgin," he murmured, as if confirming what I'd already told him.

He can see that from looking at me?

"I can see your hymen," he continued in a tone of wonder.

I put my hands over my face in pure shame.

Oh god. Could I be any more embarrassed?

When I next dared to open my eyes, he was arched over me, his lips inches from mine.

"I want your first time to be perfect, little one. And I'm not sure you're ready for me."

"Oh, I'm ready all right," I said. "I want you, Steele. I want you to be my first."

I reached for him, and he let out a deep, ragged breath as he dipped his head and kissed me.

It felt so good having him on top of me, his big cock pressing up between my legs, his arms holding me tight. He slipped a finger inside me, and I was so sensitized that it almost hurt.

"My, you are wet," he growled. He added a second finger, sliding in and out, preparing me. I shuddered and trembled. I was nervous, but I wanted him inside me so bad, it was ridiculous.

He reached over to the nightstand and took something out of the drawer. A condom.

He stripped off his underwear and his cock sprang out, even bigger than I'd remembered. Trying to fit it in my mouth had been one thing. But inside me? It looked like it could break me in half.

"I'll be gentle," he assured me. "I don't want to hurt my baby."

I tried to grasp his cock, but he caught my wrist.

"Daddy can't hold back much longer," he warned.

Instead, I watched as he rolled the condom over his thick shaft. It was an XL-size one—I knew the branding. A tremor of panic started up in my stomach. Was this going to hurt like crazy? Was I going to freak out and make a fool of myself?

But Steele didn't try to enter me. He moved down my body, kissing me all over, in a blissful trail. He kissed my pubic hair tenderly, and when his tongue made contact with my clit for the first time, my hips jerked and I just about exploded.

He licked my bud with soft, rhythmic strokes, circling around as if he knew I couldn't take too much direct pressure. It was like he already knew my body so well; understood exactly how to drive me crazy.

Tingles of pleasure began at my clit, and spread all over my core.

Before long, I was getting close, close. My pussy started to spasm, my hips bumped up and down of their own accord, and I realized I'd grabbed Steele's hair in my fists. My vision began to darken, my whole world turned soft and blurry, and—

He pulled back.

"Now," he said, his voice thick with desire. "You're going to come around Daddy's cock." He sat back on his haunches, his cock like a fire hose between his thick thighs. He pushed my knees up, spreading me wide, and he began to enter me.

Holy crap. It burned as he opened me up for the first time, breaking through the virginity I'd been saving—for him. I cried out, clutching at his arms.

He was arched over me, his jaw set like he was doing his damnedest to hold back.

"Relax, little one," he told me. "In a minute, you're going to feel real good."

He kept pushing himself inside me. It felt good, then it hurt, then it felt good again. His cock was too much for me, but I knew I hadn't taken all of it yet. My hands were braced on his shoulders, my body tense. But when he leaned forward and kissed me, I melted. The sensation of his mouth on mine was blissful and... *ohh...* suddenly, he was all the way inside me.

I tore my mouth away from him, gasping. My pussy burned like crazy, but in the midst of that was a sweet, sweet sensation. My eyes teared up.

"You okay?" he asked me, looking at me searchingly.

"Yeah." I laughed. "You took my virginity."

A look of deep satisfaction crossed his face. "I did."

Slowly, he began to move. Each thrust brought pain and pleasure, wrapping around each other until I didn't know which one was which. He was so big I felt like he could split me in two. But I also knew I would never want any other cock than his.

"You feel so good inside, baby," he murmured.

"I do?" I asked.

"Incredible. So sweet and tight. I'm so glad I'm your first."

"I'm so glad you're my first, too," I said, stroking his cheek. His words drove my arousal and suddenly, I was clenching around him. "Oh, God, I'm going to come."

"Yes, come for me, baby," he rasped. "I want to see your beautiful face when you orgasm around me for the first time. I want to feel your pussy gripping my cock—"

And I was lost.

It was less a climax than a detonation, deep inside me. An earthquake that began around his cock and finished in shockwaves of pure bliss, reaching all the way to my fingers and toes. Pink stars exploded behind my closed eyelids.

"Wow," I panted, when I was done. "That was... That was—"

Steele cut off the end of my words with a growl. He began to move a lot faster, his cock pounding into me.

Long, deep, fast thrusts, his fingers biting into my hips, his breath hot on my neck. *This* was fucking, I realized. Before, he'd been holding back, making sure it was all good for me. But now, he was taking me like he wanted to. Faster and faster he went, his biceps bunching, his hips slamming home again and again until, with a roar, he exploded, too.

He collapsed on top of me and I held him tight, running my hands all over his sweaty back.

Too soon, he pulled away and eased out of me, keeping hold of the condom as he did. "No babies," he said with a wry smile.

There was blood on the condom. And on the bed sheet. Quite a lot of it. I wasn't too surprised, but it was kind of embarrassing. "Sorry," I said.

"Nothing to apologize for," he replied, and flashed me a sexy, slightly cocky smile. He cleaned up, then he handed me some tissues and I cleaned up, too. Then he took all the mess away and climbed back into the bed, taking me in his arms.

"I'm sorry if I hurt you, babygirl," he murmured, stroking my cheek.

"It didn't hurt so much. Not compared to how good you made me feel."

His face lit with pleasure as he lowered his head and kissed me tenderly. "I'm so glad to hear that," he said.

"I'm so sleepy," I muttered a moment later as I felt myself starting to doze.

"Then go to sleep in my arms," he whispered, and I did.

CHAPTER 11

Steele

I overslept. For the first time in twenty years, my internal body clock didn't wake me, and it was light outside when I opened my eyes. Confusion blanketed my thoughts.

Then I remembered.

Carrie was asleep beside me. We'd drifted apart during the night and she was lying on her side, arms crossed over her pert little breasts, and her long eyelashes pillowed on her cheeks. She looked like a little blonde angel. I could have stayed there for hours, watching her sleep.

I had never felt this way before. I'd resisted letting Carrie into my heart—into my bed—because of Victoria. Now I wanted this moment to last forever.

But I needed to feed the animals. I crept out of bed, so I didn't wake her, and got dressed quietly.

Outside, the animals were going crazy. They thrived on

routine, and when things changed, they couldn't comprehend it. I milked the cow, then I mucked out the horses. They were skittish and impatient, and it took longer than usual. My mind, my body, were all full of last night.

Of Carrie.

Taking her virginity had been even more precious than I'd imagined. Being inside her for the first time—where no one had been before. It was the best night of my life. I couldn't believe how small and tight she was. But how wet she was as well; how her little muscles had gripped my cock eagerly, welcoming me in. That look of determination on her face, even though I knew I was hurting her. God knew I didn't want to hurt her—I wanted her first time to be the best it could be. But she was so small that it was inevitable.

Then the surprise and ecstasy on her face as she orgasmed around me. The flush on her cheeks; the feeling of her pussy spasming around my cock was something I knew I'd remember, always.

She was mine now. I'd claimed her. And nothing would come between us again.

I'd been holding out on her, because I was worried I'd lose myself.

But the truth was, I was already lost in this wild girl who wanted to call me Daddy.

Daddy.

Every time she said that word, a bolt of yearning went through my body, my cock the lightning conductor. I'd never wanted this for myself before—never thought about it. But now it was happening, it felt so right. As if my soul had been looking for it all my life. Maybe that was why I'd stayed single so long after Victoria, lived out here in isolation, waiting for the right one to come along, like a stroke of fate.

I took Rex out for a run on the rein. He was as wild as ever, but I didn't care. I had so much vigor running through me that I was equal to his feral ways, and eventually, he calmed. Maybe he sensed an affinity between us.

When I'd gotten him back in his stall, I went inside, showered, then prepared breakfast for Carrie and me. I put it on a tray and for the first time in my life, I carried it through to the bedroom.

Another one of my rules broken. I laughed to myself. If I wasn't very careful, instead of me training Carrie, she was gonna wind up converting me to her messy ways.

She stirred as I entered the room. When I set the tray down on the nightstand, her eyes fluttered open. She pulled herself up on her elbows, adorably blurred and sleepy.

Then her eyes opened wide, her face a picture of horror. "I overslept!" she exclaimed. "I'm so sorry, Steele. I don't know what happened."

I chuckled. "Don't worry, so did I."

She frowned. "I thought you said your body clock never fails you?"

"Guess something drained its batteries last night." I grinned.

She looked at me suspiciously. "You're not going to punish me for this?"

"I can hardly punish you when I did the same thing myself, can I?"

Her face filled with mischief. Then her gaze floated over to the nightstand. "Something smells real good."

"Brought you breakfast in bed to celebrate."

"Celebrate," she repeated, a shy smile tugging at her lips.

I plumped up the pillows behind her, and put the tray on her lap. Then I sat beside her and we dug in.

"Pancakes and bacon—my favorite," she said happily.

"I know, little one. I pay attention to these things."

We munched contentedly for a few minutes.

"I'm sorry I wasn't very good, you know, last night," she

said suddenly.

I stilled, my heart just about shattering in my chest. "Good? Of course you were. You were... perfect."

She pursed her lips like she didn't quite believe me.

"That was the most special night of my life. It means we're really together now. And nothing will ever change that," I told her.

"Really?" she whispered, and her face lit with hope.

"Really." I took her small hand and kissed it. "And this makes me happier than you can imagine."

"Me too. I want to be your little one, always," she said, and waves of warmth and tenderness rolled through me.

* * *

Carrie

STEELE and I worked outside all day, mainly on the cows. I felt blissed out, and giddy around him. I kept replaying what he'd said to me this morning about us really being together. It all seemed too perfect to be true. I kept thinking I'd wake up and discover I was still sleeping in a ditch—or, even worse, be back in my mom's house, with Enzo leering at me.

Was Steele really going to be my daddy forever? I was scared to get too attached to him, in case this was all just a game for him, and he got bored of me one day. But I was already getting in deep. I got butterflies every time he looked at me. I yearned to be touching him, kissing him, in his arms. I started having stupid little daydreams about our future together.

Steele and I checked on the newborns. He kept a note of the pregnancies and the births he was expecting, and said he thought there were only three more to come this season. The little calves were adorable. If they were born during the night, they had trouble standing up by themselves. Steele sprayed some disinfectant on their umbilical cords, then he rubbed them down, stood them up on their feet, and off they went to their mothers, like magic.

We also ran a sweep of the guest quarters to make sure that everything was in order. The rooms were beautiful—rustic, but real classy. When Steele told me how much it cost to stay there each night, my eyes about popped out of my head.

He laughed. "Seems crazy to me, too. Paying so much for what I do every day. But for tourists, it's an experience they can't get anywhere else."

We went through to the kitchen and checked that all the fittings functioned as they should.

"When's your brother coming back?" I asked him.

He sighed. "When he feels like it. He's in the city at the moment. Who knows, he might stay there all winter."

"The city?"

"Oh—Vancouver. Guess it doesn't mean a lot to you, huh?"

I shrugged. "I passed it on the way up here, I think."

"Folks like it. But that's because they haven't heard of Ashcroft," Steele replied with a wry smile.

"My hometown is real small," I said. "I've never really been anywhere else. Well, until... you know."

"Must've been a shock to see the world."

"If I'd had time to think about it, it would have freaked me out. But the only thing on my mind was getting as far away from Texas as I could."

"I'll take you to Vancouver one day," he said. "I think you'll like it." Then he frowned.

"What is it?"

"Maybe you'll like it too much and I'll lose you to the big city."

I grinned. "No chance. Where I am is just about perfect."

Impulsively, he took my hand, and didn't let it go until we got back to the horses. I loved the way my hand got enveloped in his big, thick fingers. Loved the masculine roughness of his skin.

I felt stupidly happy. Still scared, but I decided to quit worrying and take him at his word.

My body was sore from yesterday—inside and out—but I couldn't wait for him to fuck me again. To make me his.

* * *

IN THE EARLY EVENING, I'd just finished showering when Steele said, "Go up to the barn and bring down that dress of yours, and your new shoes."

I opened my mouth to ask why.

"Just do it," he said. He seemed restless, a little wired.

Was this a new game of his? I wondered as I brought the pretty pink dress, shoes and pantyhose down from the loft.

"Go put them on," he said, "and make your hair look nice."

I went into the bedroom and got dressed up and brushed my hair so it sat neatly on my shoulders. Wispy as it was, there wasn't a whole lot I could do with it. Whether I blow-dried it or let it dry naturally, it just hung around my face.

I looked at my reflection in the closet mirror and did a double take.

The dress looked the same as when I'd tried it on in the store, but somehow, *I* looked different. I scrutinized my face. Something in my eyes, maybe. They seemed to have a new sparkle.

And then I remembered, and my stomach gave a little jump.

Maybe it was because I was no longer a virgin. Because Steele had made love to me for the first time. I took a deep breath in and out, waves of bliss flowing through me.

My daddy had made me his. And we'd always be together. I wouldn't be alone or scared anymore. My heart lit up like it was wrapped in fairy lights.

I skipped back to the kitchen to see what Steele had in mind.

He emerged from the bathroom, wearing just a towel. He smelled of aqua cologne, and the sight of his bare torso filled me with yearning.

As he took me in, his eyes glowed with pleasure. "Even prettier than I remember," he said. "Give me a twirl."

Obediently, I held my hands out to the sides and spun around, like a little girl.

His eyes crinkled at the corners. "What a little princess you are," he said.

And in that moment, I did feel like a princess.

"Just hang here a second," he called, and headed to the bedroom.

In a couple of minutes he was back, in a pair of blue denim jeans and a crisp, blue-and-white striped button-down. He looked more handsome than ever. *He's mine—my daddy*, I thought, and my heart flipped.

He took hold of both my hands. "Ready to go?"

I frowned. "Go where?

"Out to dinner, of course."

Now my heart leaped like a bounding rabbit. He was taking me out for dinner—on a real date. I'd never been on a grown-up date before. Dating at high school usually meant hanging out by the bleachers or at the mall. But this was an official date, with a grown-up man.

Steele always had great manners, but I felt like he was making a special effort to act like a gentleman tonight. He opened the truck door for me, and when we arrived at the restaurant, he took my hand and helped me step down onto the sidewalk. I felt like a princess in a beautiful fairytale, hand in hand with her daddy.

The restaurant looked fancy, with white tablecloths and candles. As we entered, I felt stiff, worried I was going to do something dumb and embarrass myself.

As if sensing my discomfort, Steele stroked my palm in soothing circles, and I instantly calmed.

He'd reserved a table by the window. It was beautiful and so romantic. The candle flickered between us, highlighting the planes of Steele's handsome face, and glowing in his eyes —eyes that were looking at me with approval and desire. I felt light-headed and giggly with all the emotions welling up inside me.

But just as we'd settled at the table, someone called Steele's name. He got up and looked around. The voice was coming from a couple sitting at the table behind us.

"Hi, guys!" Steele replied. Then he took my hand and led me over. "I'd like to introduce you to my date, Carrie. Carrie, meet two dear friends of mine, Barbara and Tom."

The couple got up and shook my hand enthusiastically. They were around Steele's age, or maybe a couple of years younger. Tom had a cowboy style, and an open, friendly face, and Barbara was pretty and outdoorsy looking, with curly brown hair. "It's a pleasure to meet you, Carrie," she said, her eyes sparkling.

"You too," I replied shyly, still choking at the words *my date*. It was official.

"Come join us here," Tom said. "There's enough space at the table for two more chairs."

"Oh no, I'll get out of you folks' hair," Steele replied.

I looked at him, sensing he was being kind.

"Let's join them," I said. "It'll be fun."

His brow furrowed. "Are you sure?"

"Of course."

Steele touched my back in a little gesture of gratitude. "Okay, great," he said.

Practical as ever, he grabbed two chairs from a nearby table and set them out for us, then the server came over to take our drinks order. Right away, I ordered a Coke. Then Tom asked if everyone wanted to split a bottle of wine, and I felt like a kid. But the truth was, I didn't really like the taste of alcohol.

"You have what you want, honey," Steele murmured close to my ear.

I flashed him a grateful smile, and my stomach gave a little jump. I no longer found it eerie that he often guessed my thoughts—he was my daddy, so of course he knew what was on my mind.

I tasted the wine when it came. It was just as sour as I'd expected. Steele laughed at my attempts not to make a face, and threw me an indulgent look. I pushed the glass away, glad to stick with my cola.

Once we'd ordered the starter and entrées, Barbara launched into conversation. She was very talkative, and drew me into her life on the farm she and Tom ran together. It turned out they were Steele's neighbors, two ranches away, and they bred show horses. She said people came from all over Canada to buy them.

"Drop by and see them any time," she told me. "I always love company." I soon felt like I'd known her for years. Tom wasn't as talkative, but he had a mischievous sense of humor.

Barbara asked what had brought me to Canada. Thinking fast, I told them I was a trainee cowgirl and I'd gotten bored of the heat in the South. They seem to accept what I was saying without question.

"It's so great to meet you, Carrie," Barbara told me

halfway through the starter. "I'm always saying to Steele it's high time he got himself a wife."

Wife?

A judder of electricity went through me. I opened my mouth and closed it again. Could a man be a daddy and husband at the same time? It was all so new and confusing. I decided it was something I'd have to ask about later.

Tom jabbed his index finger at Steele. "Y'know, Steele likes acting out the whole lone cowboy thing, but he's really a sociable guy," he told me. "Always thought it was a shame you've been isolating yourself from the world at that old ranch of yours."

Steele laughed. "I'd hardly call it isolation. Half the year, I've got guests and employees coming out my ears."

Barbara fixed him with a serious look. "You know what he means, Steele." She turned her attention to me. "And I've never seen him so happy, my dear." This time, there was a twinkle in her eye.

A little glow lit in my chest. Was that really true? I'd been focusing on what Steele was doing to take care of me. But was my presence in his life really bringing him happiness? I sure hoped so. Under the table, I reached for his thigh and squeezed it. He laid his hand on top of mine, and flashed me a secret smile. *Yes*, it meant. And my heart opened right up, like a blooming flower.

The food was delicious. We all had steaks for entrée, and when the dessert list came, I really wanted ice cream, but was worried they'd think it was immature so I ordered crème caramel instead.

At the end of the meal, we left with warm goodbyes and plans to meet up the following week.

Outside, Steele slipped his arm around my shoulders. "Thank you," he said in a low voice.

"For what?"

"For sacrificing our date to meet my friends."

"I had fun with them," I told him.

He chuckled and dabbed the tip of my nose. "They had fun too, I could tell."

"They liked me?"

"Of course they did."

"They didn't think of me as just a kid?"

"No, you acted real grown up. You were a credit to me, babygirl."

As I climbed into the car, I gave a little skip of joy.

The truth was, I'd always enjoyed the company of older people. I found my schoolmates kind of immature. The way they were obsessed with their images, the way they never put their phones down, and made stupid jokes about sex.

I liked feeling little when it was just me and Steele, but in public, it was much better being a grown-up—as long as I had Steele to take care of me.

* * *

WHEN WE GOT HOME, Steele started to undress me.

"Daddy, I'm not sure if I can. I'm kind of sore—" I began, but he shushed me.

"We're just going to bathe you today, and tomorrow we'll see how things are," he reassured me.

He ran me a bath and poured a ton of salt in. Then he made me soak for a good long while.

After all the food and excitement, and the hot bath, I was real sleepy. I barely had enough energy to brush my teeth before Steele led me to the bedroom. He peeled back the coverlet on my side of the bed and made a show of tucking me in before he snuck in the other side, and curled himself around me. The last thing I was aware of was him murmuring sweet words in my ear.

CHAPTER 12

Carrie

The next day, it was raining when we got up and it didn't let up all morning. Working at the chores was miserable, and Steele seemed tense and distracted. When we came back to the house, he seemed to have his own personal rain cloud hanging over his head.

"What is it?" I asked him.

"What's what?"

"This mood you've been in all morning." I was disappointed and a little hurt because I'd woken up full of excitement at spending the day with him, but he was acting like he didn't want any company.

He yanked his cowboy hat off and sighed heavily. "Oh, nothing, nothing." He put his arms around me and hugged me.

"I'm sorry, I just had some business stuff on my mind. I shouldn't let it distract me."

He rubbed my back, and soon his hands began to wander over my body. When he cupped my ass, he gave a sigh of need.

"How's that pussy of yours?" he murmured.

"Uh, it's better," I said with a nervous laugh. "Mostly."

"Let me take a look," he said.

"No," I squeaked, before I had time to think. "It's fine."

"Carrie." His voice was a low, warning growl. "Take your panties down and show me your pussy."

Hot waves of embarrassment flowed through me. "No, I'm shy."

He slipped his hand between my legs. Not hard, just cupping me. "Who does this belong to?"

I gulped. "It's yours," I whispered. And I burned with a mixture of shame and arousal.

"Whose?" he said, much louder.

"Yours," I repeated. "...Daddy."

He let out a slow, satisfied breath. "That's right, it's mine, so I get to see it whenever I want."

He unfastened my jeans and yanked them down, along with my panties, until they were bunched around my ankles. Then he flipped me backward onto the couch and pushed my legs up, over my head, so I was bent in half like a pretzel. Most humiliatingly of all, he grabbed the swing-arm lamp that sat near the edge of the couch and trained its head on me. His big forearm pressed down on my thighs and he held me in position, keeping me still while he examined me.

I squirmed and flailed, but could barely move a muscle. He'd gotten me pinned down as efficiently as a butterfly on a corkboard.

When he touched my outer lips, I stifled a moan. He spread them apart and peered at my entrance.

"You're a little bruised right here," he commented. I did feel bruised, and maybe even a little torn from the intrusion of his huge cock—from him taking my virginity. "Mmm... I think it'll be one more day until you're ready for me again," he said in a thoughtful tone, and a rush of heat spread from my chest to my cheeks.

He released me and my legs dropped back down to the ground. "You can pull up your panties now," he said. "But know this: disobeying me like that has just earned you a punishment, young lady."

Warmth spread through me and I waited for him to continue, but he didn't. With a wink, he headed outdoors, whistling, and left me to get dressed.

ALL AFTERNOON, I prickled with nerves, wondering what the punishment was going to be.

When Steele got back from milking the cows, he seemed to have decided.

"Take your clothes off and leave them in the bedroom," he told me.

"All of them?" I enquired, although I already knew what the answer was going to be.

He gave a curt nod. I retreated to the bedroom and undressed completely. When I shuffled back into the hallway, fighting the urge to cover my body with my hands, Steele was bringing an old plastic chair in from outside. I watched anxiously as he took it into the bathroom and set it in the bathtub. *What the heck is he planning to do now?* My innocent brain clearly lacked the imagination to guess.

As many colors as the rainbow.

"Come sit down," he said, and I felt relief. Daddy would tell me what to do; I could just obey.

I clambered into the tub and sat down awkwardly, and then he told me to spread my legs.

I'd learned my lesson. I did exactly as he told me, pulling my knees to my chest and holding them wide apart. I was still as embarrassed as hell for him to see me like that, but I guessed I was going to have to get used to it.

"I'm going to shave you, babygirl," he told me, a hint of a smile hovering around his stern mouth. "That'll teach you that you can't go hiding from me."

"What—" I opened my mouth to argue. My legs automatically inched closed. I'd never shaved my pubic hair off before.

He took a man's razor from the cupboard and some shaving foam, and I started to tremble. What if his hand slipped and he cut me? There wasn't a whole lot of margin for error down there.

"Easy, babygirl," he murmured, rubbing my leg. "I'd never do anything to hurt you."

I relaxed slightly. "Have you done this before?"

He paused, still stroking my bare thigh. "Yes," he finally answered. "A long time ago."

I wanted to ask who it was with, but the words died as he picked up the shaving cream can.

"What if your hand slips?" I asked in a quavery voice.

"I've got a steady hand," he assured me as he squirted foam over my mons and knelt at my feet.

It felt weird, and I think I held my breath the entire time, but he was real gentle. He shaved off the triangle at the top first. Then he made sure the delicate skin of my labia was taut before running the sharp blade over it, and he didn't nick me once.

By the end, I was breathing hard. Warmth pooled in the pit of my belly at the reverent way Steele stroked my labia, checking for rough patches. Judging by the tightness in his jeans, he was affected too.

When he was done, he instructed me to get on my hands

and knees. He spread my cheeks and ran the razor along my ass crack as well. Then he turned on the shower, checked the water was nice and warm, and rinsed me clean.

"Beautiful," he said. "And we're going to keep it like that from now on."

Excitement curled through me. The way he gently but firmly took care of me set a fire burning in my belly.

He took a towel and carefully patted me dry. "Go ahead and feel it," he told me when he was finished. While he watched, I ran my hand shyly over my pussy. The whole area was silky smooth. I was startled at how soft it felt.

He straightened up. "Now, you're going to stay naked for the rest of the day." He looked thoughtful. "Maybe even the rest of the week, until you've learned your lesson. Until you've learned that you can't go hiding anything from Daddy."

He left me alone in the bathroom, and I dried the rest of my body off.

Is he really expecting me to walk around the house naked?

Apparently. I'd already learned that if he said something, he meant it. The thought made me feel all squirmy and embarrassed. I hung the towel back up. Then I took the chair, put in front of the mirror, and stood on it so I could look at myself.

At the sight of my bare pussy, my cheeks went hot. I was so exposed. It was pink, with only a little bit of my inner lips peeping out. I guessed it was pretty.

"Carrie?" came Steele's voice through the door.

I jumped. Hurriedly, I stuffed the chair back into the bathtub and opened the door. *Wow.* I suddenly felt ten times as exposed now.

Steele's eyes filled with desire. He went to me and kissed me deeply. His hands ran up and down my back, moved down to my ass, and finished by cupping my breasts, his thumbs chafing at my nipples.

"You're so beautiful and sexy, baby," he whispered. "It's going to drive me crazy seeing you like that all night."

"Same," I murmured, because the ache between my legs was growing inside me again.

Steele had pulled all the curtains closed and turned the heat up, and for the rest of the evening, he did seem to be intent on driving himself crazy—stroking me, kissing me, absently grabbing my boob or caressing my pussy as he passed me in the kitchen. It was kind of objectifying, but hot as hell. I was *his*, I reminded myself. He could touch me anywhere and any time he wanted. I ate dinner naked; I stacked the dishwasher naked. And all the while, Steele's eyes were on me, burning into me, his cock swollen beneath his zipper. I was ridiculously turned on. Still too broken to take him, but wanting him like crazy all the same.

"Finish cleaning up," he ordered.

"Then what?" I asked, hoping he'd tell me how the evening would end.

"Do as I say, babygirl." He raised a brow and pinched my ass.

I jumped and hustled to obey. I could have hummed, I was so excited. But then I had a thought. "Daddy..."

"Yes, girl?"

The sternness in his voice made me squirmy. "Um, have you done this before? With another girl?"

There was a long pause. I kept my eyes down, scrubbing at a sticky patch on the counter with a dishrag.

When Steele spoke close behind me, I jumped. He put a hand on my back to calm me. "I had a lover once. She and I did a lot of the stuff we're doing. But it wasn't the same."

I turned around, needing to see his face. He looked

thoughtful. I bit my lip, wondering if he was remembering his past lover. Was she better in bed than me?

Probably.

He cupped my chin, smoothing my lip with his rough thumb. "I'm glad I found you."

His deep voice made me melt. "You mean I found you," I corrected, because I knew it'd rile him up.

He growled and dropped his hand, turning me back to the sink and smacking my ass. "Back to work."

When I'd finished wiping the kitchen down, he called me to come over to him.

He was sitting on the couch, and he took a cushion and dropped it on the floor between his legs.

"Kneel down here, little one," he told me.

I did as he said, quivering with anticipation. He wanted me to suck his cock. I was nervous because I knew I wasn't very good at it, but I was eager to have him in my mouth again. Maybe, with practice, I could get as good as his other lover.

"You're going to suck Daddy's cock," he said, his voice low and crooning. He pulled his zipper down and I watched, mesmerized, as he took it out. It was rock-hard—but I knew that already from the way his pants had been tenting all night.

"I want to feel your mouth around me." He took my head in his hands and drew me closer, and I licked my lips, readying myself for him. The thought of Steele's former lover reared up in my mind. Was she older, more experienced? Would I ever be better than her?

Steele coaxed my head down, and I focused on pleasing him. It wasn't much easier than last time. He was so big, and every time his cock slid toward the back of my tongue, I gagged hard. It was so embarrassing.

"Take your time, little one," he urged me, but it was no

good. Tears sprang to my eyes—part shame, part discomfort —but he kept going, holding my head, thrusting in and out, pausing every time I choked on him. I tried my best, desperate to pleasure him; to make him satisfied with me.

I wanted so much to be the best babygirl I could for him.

But, before I knew what I was doing, my hand had sneaked down between my legs, and I started to touch myself.

Soon, Steele figured out what was going on. "Does sucking my cock turn you on, babygirl?" he asked in a husky voice.

I nodded, my mouth too full of him to speak.

He groaned. "You can touch yourself. I want to see you come."

But as soon as he said that, I got shy, and I couldn't concentrate on rubbing my clit and sucking him at the same time. Eventually, he lifted me up and laid me on the sofa. Then he spread my legs and went down on me.

His tongue was soft and skillful, and I shuddered and trembled as he drove my arousal, bringing me closer and closer to the brink. I imagined being able to take him as deep as he wanted, imagined him fucking me again.

An intense shudder welled up in me and suddenly, an orgasm hit me, as bright and sharp as a shard of glass. I shook from head to toe.

When I was done, he pulled me up, pushed his cock back into my mouth, and worked his hand up and down his shaft at the same time. A moment later, his hot, salty cum splashed over my tongue, and I swallowed fast.

"Good girl," he said, stroking my face. "You did good."

I nodded, warming at the praise.

I'd do better next time, I promised myself. I'd suck him like a practiced lover, not an inexperienced one.

CHAPTER 13

Steele

*L*ow, gray cloud rolled toward the horizon the next day as I drove through the dirt roads connecting a bunch of farms and ranches in the valley. I was on my way to my buddy Joel's ranch to help him put a new roof on his barn.

It often got stormy this time of year as the cold pushed its way in. I hoped there'd be more than a handful of fine days left this year—days when it wouldn't be too cold for Carrie and I to continue her training in the barn. But maybe by the time winter came along, she'd be fully trained, and I wouldn't need to discipline her anymore.

At the thought, my gut tightened. Would there come a time when she didn't need to feel my hand on her ass? I didn't like that idea at all. The passenger seat beside me was empty, and the truth was, I missed my wild little girl already. I'd been tempted to bring her along with me, but decided she needed time by herself to process the last few days. And I was well aware that I wouldn't get any work done if she was there. Instead, I'd told her to relax, and read or watch TV. She didn't need to work on the ranch while I was gone.

It had been so hard to leave her this morning, when all I wanted to do was stay in bed and take her a second time.

Her inexperienced mouth on my cock last night had blown my mind—so small, and soft, and eager. How she'd swallowed me down without making a face.

I'd woken up with a massive boner, which I'd had to take care of in the shower. She was snuggled in my arms, and it wouldn't have been difficult to turn her over and push myself into her sweet pussy. But I didn't want to rush things. I wanted to make sure that every single time was perfect for her.

Tonight, I'd take her to bed as soon as I got home, I promised myself. And I'd make her come and come until she was begging me to stop.

I whistled to myself as I drove. Carrie had gotten under my skin. That smart sassy mouth of hers. Her wildness and curiosity. The way her whole face changed when I made her submit to me. The way she was so full of gratitude for every little thing I did for her—and in future, she'd learn that there was nothing I wouldn't do for her. That I'd take care of her, no matter what. There were so many things I want to show her, to teach her.

She was such a mixture of sweetness and defiance. I never knew what to expect from her. One minute, she'd be stacking the dishwasher obediently, sneaking glances at me when she thought I wasn't looking, to check I was satisfied with her progress. The next minute, she'd act out, almost as if she wanted me to spank her. She was new to this, and a bit of a brat. It was natural for her to push boundaries.

I could tell that Tom and Barbara had liked her, too. I had

been worried they'd raise their eyebrows when they saw how young she was, but they'd acted like us being together was natural, and that reassured me. Carrie had acted so grown up, even doing her best to drink some wine. I smiled at the memory of her little face puckering in distaste. Well, I liked seeing her drinking cola; doing childish things. Whatever made her feel good. I had a hunch that she'd missed out on a lot of her childhood. I hoped I could provide her with a safe place to be whoever she needed to be at this point in her life.

She made my heart sing. It had been still before I met her —as still and calm as a lake. But now my depths were coming to the surface. And I liked that feeling, even though it scared me a little. It made me feel alive; like nothing else mattered.

Even my brother being a dick—well, more of a dick than usual—didn't bother me. He was pressuring me yet again to buy him out of the ranch. He kept saying I owed it to him, but he didn't grasp that I literally didn't have the money. He wanted me to get a mortgage on the property, but my daddy always taught us not to take on any debt, unless it was an emergency. And satisfying the whims of my lazy brother didn't classify as an emergency in my book.

Our endless conflicts occupied a lot of my thinking time, but Carrie always made me feel better. One look at her sweet face, and nothing else mattered. My little angel.

The sign for Joel's ranch came into view. When I turned into the yard, he was waiting for me, hat pushed back on his forehead as usual, and the sleeves of his plaid shirt ripped off to display his pumped up biceps and tattoos. He broke into his easy smile, and bounded over and clapped me on the back.

"Thanks for coming, dude," he said.

"Anytime," I replied, and meant it. We had a thing going on in the valley where if a neighbor asked for help, we dropped whatever was non-essential, and helped them out. One of the many things I loved about my hometown.

Joel's place was a lot messier than mine. He didn't take in guests, so he didn't have the same obligation to keep it all tidy. I kind of wished I could do away with the guests myself. If I bought my brother out, I didn't know what I'd do with them. There was no way I could run the lodgings myself. I'd probably scare half of them away with my abrupt manners. It would sure be a shame to squander all those nice buildings, though, as well as the reputation we'd built up over the years. Maybe I'd have to get someone in to manage it or something.

Joel talked me through the work we were going to do on the roof. Turned out he just wanted to put a new waterproof covering on the existing layer.

"Seems pretty straightforward," I said, and we got to work. I was glad for the opportunity to make something. As much as I loved working with the horses and cows, it was good to have a little variety sometimes.

"Heard you've got yourself a girlfriend," Joel commented as he passed a length of tarp across a corner of the roof.

"She's not my girlfriend," I grunted, before I could stop myself.

Joel pushed his hat further back on his head so he could see me better. "No?" The corners of his mouth tugged up with mischief. "Barb says she's a lovely young woman. Her words." He laughed carelessly, but I was all tensed up.

Girlfriend wasn't the right word for what I had with Carrie. But what was I supposed to call her?

Joel had stopped what he was doing and was watching me expectantly.

"Girl," I said at last. "Carrie is my girl."

Joel gave me a knowing smile. "I've always wanted that dynamic for myself, to tell you the truth. You're a lucky man."

I gave a curt nod and carried on working. What did he

know of this dynamic? I wondered. Obviously I was a lot older than Carrie, but had he sensed that I was disciplining her? I wished I could discuss this openly with him. I wondered how badly things could go wrong if I was mistaken and he freaked out. Folks in these parts were good-hearted, but they could be a little conservative.

"Have you ever had a babygirl yourself?" I asked at last.

"Yeah." Joel shrugged. "A couple. None that I've got to stick around, though. It takes a special kind of girl to appreciate the value of discipline."

"Sure does," I agreed, thinking of Victoria. I'd thought she was the perfect submissive, but now I wasn't so sure. Maybe more of her behavior had been an act than I realized. Compared with Carrie, Victoria was more experienced, but my old submissive had been calculated; jaded. I'd take Carrie's innocent pouts over Victoria's practiced ones any day. My babygirl was completely without guile.

When we were done fixing the barn roof, and it had a beautiful new waterproof covering that would last the winter, Joel insisted on taking me to town for a thank-you lunch.

We had burgers and beers, and as the alcohol loosened me up, I started to tell him a little bit about how I'd been training Carrie. None of the most intimate details—just the overall concept.

He leaned forward, listening attentively. "Sounds like about the best thing I could imagine," he said. "Finding a woman who matches your desires is like winning Olympic gold." He took a long swig of his beer. "Hope I'll be lucky like that one day. Although, out here, I'm hardly beating them off with a stick."

"Olympic gold," I repeated. "Couldn't have put it better myself."

Grinning, he raised his beer and we clinked bottles.

"You're a great guy, Joel. You'll find the right one for you," I told him.

We wound up talking for a long time, and it was almost dusk by the time I got back to the ranch. I was excited to see Carrie, my heart beating faster as I pulled into the yard. I was going to take her straight to bed, to make up for lost time. The windows of the ranch house emitted a welcoming glow. It had never looked so homely, I thought. I wondered what she was doing right now—watching TV snuggled up in bed, or maybe doing her nails or reading up on horseback riding.

I slowed my pace as I walked up the path to the front porch, savoring the moment when I would lay eyes on her. As I stepped onto the decking, I saw through the window that she was on the couch, looking at something on the laptop. But when I opened the door, she slammed it shut, and a guilty look flashed across her face.

"Hi, little one," I said.

"Hi, Daddy!" She leaped up, ran over to me, and wrapped her arms around my waist, before laying her head on my chest.

I hugged her tight, my heart melting.

"How did it go?" She tipped her head up to look at me, and I planted a kiss on her sweet cherry lips. She gave a small sigh of appreciation. I loved that she enjoyed our kisses as much as I did.

"Went well," I said. "Didn't take so long once we got into it." I went over to the couch and sat down.

She was bouncing around with a nervous energy. "I made some iced tea," she told me. "Wanna try it?"

I frowned. "I've never tried iced tea in my life."

"I wanted to give you a taste of my home."

I grinned. "Yes, of course. I'd love to try your iced tea, baby."

She skipped over to the fridge excitedly, and I was glad I'd said the right thing. Such little things made her happy.

She handed me a glass of the light brown, transparent liquid. "I didn't make it too sweet. I know not everyone likes it."

I tasted it. "Nice," I said.

She shrugged self-consciously. "Might take some getting used to."

"The best things often do," I commented. She caught my eye with a mischievous glance as she picked up on the secondary meaning.

I lifted my arm and she automatically snuggled against my body. We fit together as if we'd sat like that a hundred times before. I couldn't still couldn't believe we'd only known each other for a few days. I was starting to feel like we'd always been together.

"What did you do today?" I asked her.

"Oh, I went to talk to Megan for a bit. Don't worry, I didn't try to ride her or anything crazy like that. Then I went for a walk around the fields, said hi to a few of the horses. Then I watched Netflix. Then I took a bath. Then I watched Netflix some more."

There was a catch in her voice when she got to the last item on the list, and her eyes shifted back and forth. Something stirred in my gut. Old memories of Victoria, looking shifty as she brushed off my questions. Was Carrie lying to me?

"Guess we'd better go milk the cow," I said, putting my empty glass on the coffee table. "You go first, and I'll catch you up."

"Sure thing." She got to her feet and did exactly what I'd told her.

As soon as she was gone, I grabbed the laptop and went to her search history.

If she'd been using incognito mode, I'd have been stumped. I didn't have the technology know-how to get past that. But she hadn't. Her search history was right there. Naughty girl.

When I saw what Carrie had been looking at, my gut dropped like an elevator in freefall. The porn site loaded immediately, with its obscene images and ads blinking at me.

I scanned the page, and as I did, a pop up chat appeared in its own little window.

"Hey, girl, where'd you go?" The message was the last of several, from a huge dude named Cyrus X. BigCock. His avatar was a picture of a waxed torso with a sleek set of abs.

She'd been chatting with him while I was gone. Something inside me died. *Victoria all over again.*

I scrolled up, feeling sick. Carrie had initiated the chat. "I need to know how to give a blow job," she'd typed.

"You like giving head, sexy girl?"

"Yes. My daddy likes it too. Can you give me tips?"

"Send me nudes, and I will." The last thing he sent was a dick pic.

Anger and dismay boiled in my veins like lava. I tore open the front door, and stormed out to the cow stall.

When I arrived there, Carrie was already milking the cow, sitting down on the stool, just like I'd taught her; making little splashing noises as she managed to squeeze the milk into the pail. I set my jaw. Not now. I'd wait until she was done, and I was calm enough to think how best to handle this. What had prompted this epic betrayal?

Fighting to stay calm, I went over and checked her technique, and gave a hint on how to use her hand most efficiently on the cow's thick teats. Then I went and checked on the horses, making sure they had enough hay for the night.

When Carrie came back into the house, she showed me the full bottles of milk triumphantly. "I fed the cow and washed everything up and secured the door," she announced. "You won't even need to check on me. I made sure everything was perfect."

I took the milk and inspected it. The jug was as full, as usual. "Good girl," I told her. "Now, take off your clothes."

She blinked. "What?"

"I said, take off your clothes. It's time for your next training session."

Her face fell. "Training? Now?"

Still playing innocent.

I worked my jaw back and forth. "Did you really think you'd get away with hiding something from me? I thought we were past all that."

She shook her head, forehead puckered in confusion.

I'd been hoping she'd confess right away. But obviously I hadn't gotten that stubbornness out of her yet.

"Carrie?" I said in a warning voice, fixing her with a hard stare.

Defiance blazed in her eyes. Was she really going to disobey me?

"Okay then," she said in a sulky tone and lifted the hem of her T-shirt. To my delight, she wasn't wearing a bra today. But I kept my face impassive as she pulled the T-shirt over her head, revealing her soft caramel nipples, then took down her jeans, and finally, reluctantly, her panties. My breath caught in my throat the sight of her neatly shaved pussy, so pink and perfect, bared to my gaze. Her sweet sex would look so good, gripping my cock. Meanwhile, her nipples were already hardening to little peaks that I would enjoy taking in my mouth later.

She looked at me, hands held loosely by her sides, knowing better than to hide her body from me. *Good.* At least that was one thing she'd learned by now. There was hope in her eyes—hope that I would take her to bed and make love to her tenderly. That would come later, too.

But not until I'd taught her one hell of a lesson.

"Okay, we're going to the barn," I told her. "You first."

The hope dropped away from her face. "I-it's cold out there," she stuttered.

"I don't care. This is part of your punishment." I watched her face as I said the word *punishment*, to see if she was figuring out that I knew. But her face betrayed nothing.

Slowly, reluctantly, she went to the front door, opened it, and stepped outside.

It was cool, an evening breeze blowing, and she shivered.

"Hands by your sides," I barked.

She began to walk fast. I followed close behind, enjoying the sight of her naked in the outdoors, her pert little rear jiggling a little as she scuttled along. I was very much looking forward to punishing it.

When we got inside the barn, she was shivering. I shut the door, and turned on the light. "Come here," I told her.

I stood her in front of me and gave her a rough rubdown, like I often did with the horses, bringing the blood back to the surface of her skin. Gradually, the shivering stopped and her gooseflesh was transformed into soft, silky skin again.

I led her to the side wall of the barn, where a series of hooks were attached, six or so feet off the ground. "Stand right there," I told her. "Face to the wall."

Her forehead puckered again, but she obeyed, standing so close that her nipples grazed the wooden boards.

Good.

I went over to the pile of leather equipment I'd left laid out on the hay bale, and selected some straps. I looped one strap around her right wrist and one around her left, and secured the other ends to hooks, stretching her arms wide apart.

Then I attached straps around each ankle, and pulled her legs wide, too. She gasped at the sensation of being spread like that.

I connected the straps to a pair of floor hooks, then stood back and admired my handiwork.

Carrie was tightly bound, totally vulnerable to me, and she had no idea what was coming next. I retrieved the riding crop from the hay bale and, as I walked back to her, slapping the leather keeper across my palm, she turned her head, trying to look at me over her left shoulder.

She wouldn't forget this lesson in a hurry.

CHAPTER 14

Carrie

*S*lap. *Slap. Slap,* went the whip in Steele's hand. I cringed at the memory of its sting on my flesh. Pointlessly, I tugged at the leather straps binding my wrists and ankles, but they held me firm. Clearly I wasn't going anywhere, until Steele let me.

I felt as vulnerable as hell like this, all stretched out and helpless. My boobs were pressed against the cold wall, while my back was arched and my ass was spread, fully displaying me to Steele.

Slap, slap, slap, went the whip again.

"I thought we were making progress in your training, Carrie. But obviously not," he growled.

Crap. He sounded mad. Madder than ever before.

I opened my mouth and closed it again, unsure if a response was required.

"You disappointed me, Carrie," he continued.

"Why?" I said in a quiet voice, but the truth was beginning to dawn on me. I'd been good all of last night and all of today, except for that *one little thing*.

He took another step toward me, and began to stroke the leather tip of the crop over my body—from my wrists to my shoulders; down the center of my back; then from my ankles to my inner thighs. It was soft at first, tickling, innocuous, but I knew it wouldn't stay that way for long.

Suddenly, he grabbed the hair at the nape of my neck and yanked my head toward him.

"I think you know why," he growled.

Shit. He looked not just mad, but disappointed in me, which was worse than anything. His eyes blazed with a cold fire, and I swallowed hard.

He stepped back and brought the crop down on my still tender flesh. I yelped.

"Shhh," he crooned. "I don't want to hear a whimper from you until I ask you another question."

Crack!

The crop came down again, on my left cheek this time. It stung like crazy, but I sucked my lips in and clenched my jaw, forcing myself to stay quiet.

He whipped my sore ass six more times, then he moved on to my thighs, swatting them harder with every stroke, edging closer and closer to my spread pussy.

When the crop touched me right there, I jerked hard. I could barely move though—there was virtually no give in the straps.

He tapped my pussy a few more times. "Hmmm..." he murmured.

I was wet; I sensed it; heard the tacky sound it made against the crop. He pressed the length of the crop against my crack, and I suppressed a moan.

"Aroused by your punishment, again," he commented.

He took a step back and was silent. The only sound was the slapping of the crop against his palm. I trembled. The wooden slats suddenly felt abrasive against my face, and my arms started to ache from being above my head.

What was he thinking? Planning?

He went to the wrist straps and unfastened them roughly, as if he was annoyed. He unhooked my ankles, too.

"Turn around," he ordered.

I did as he said and he tied me up again, but facing him this time. I couldn't work out if that was better or worse.

He ran the crop over my body again, as I'd seen him do with Rex—testing his limbs, getting him accustomed to being touched.

The end of the crop went over my right nipple, then over my left. I shuddered as they pebbled painfully. Then he stroked it up my inner thighs, right then left, then over my bare pussy. Up and down my slit it went, spreading my wetness all over. He gave it a few taps, each one harder than the last, until they truly stung. Still, I pressed my lips together and managed not to make a sound.

"Tell me..." He pressed the crop under my chin, forcing me to raise my head. "Why do I come home from a hard day's work, go check my emails, and discover that while I've been hammering roofs, you've been chatting with another man? A *pornstar?*" He spat the word out with disgust.

Heat flooded my face. *Crap.* He had seen the chat. I knew that had been a mistake—but I'd hoped he would never find out. I'd been praying he was mad about something else.

"I'm disappointed in you, Carrie. Did you not enjoy having sex with me?"

"Y-yes, of course I did. I-it was amazing," I stuttered.

"Did you enjoy it too much? Did you need more—from another man?"

"It wasn't that. It was—" I broke off as the crop whistled through the air and slapped my inner thigh, hard.

I yelped. While I was still mid yell, Steele aimed a slap on the left side, too.

"*What* was it? What possible reason would you have for chatting up men on the Internet?"

He drew back the crop and this time, unbelievably, aimed it at my left breast.

"Oww! Shit!" I cried out, as much in outrage as pain.

"Language," he snapped. His jaw was set in that stern way of his, but hurt glimmered in his eyes.

He's hurt. I hurt him. The pain of realizing that was way worse than the crop. I hung my head. I deserved this punishment. I deserved way worse.

"What's your safeword?" he asked.

"Strawberry."

"That's right, girl. Use it if you need to."

I clenched my jaw. He wouldn't hear it. Not tonight.

He aimed a lash at my right breast, then the left again. It hurt like crazy. It was ten times worse than being beat on my ass or thighs. He kept going, one after the other, after the other, until I was so stunned by the pain that I'd forgotten what the question was. And then he whipped me right across my nipple. A blast of pure agony exploded in my head, and I squirmed. I yanked at the straps, desperate to find a way to protect myself, despite the fact I was spread out and completely vulnerable to him.

Slap! went the crop again, and a point of fire exploded in my left nipple. Then he moved down, faster and faster, criss-crossing my thighs, my stomach, then back up to my breasts again. My body was on fire with a million burning stings, like I'd face-planted into a nest of ants.

"Stop, please stop!" I begged him over and over. I was dimly aware that I was sobbing, that my cheeks were drenched in tears. The safeword hovered at the edges of my mind, but I was far away from yielding to it. I could take this punishment. I deserved it.

And then I couldn't.

The crop whistled through the air and landed on my clit. All the ants in the world bit me right there. I screamed like a banshee.

"I was trying to learn!" I wailed.

"What?"

"I was trying to learn how to give head properly," I muttered, shame burning in my chest.

He'd frozen, his hand drawn back, ready to whip me again. "That's why you were chatting with a porn star?" he repeated in an incredulous tone.

I nodded. "I was so embarrassed at how bad I was yesterday. The girls at school used to boast about how deep they could go. I just thought if I watched porn and talked with a guy about it, I could learn some techniques. So next time I give you head, I won't disappoint you."

Steele's hand dropped to his side, and he blinked several times. "Why do you think you disappointed me?"

"Because I was so bad, you stopped me and jacked yourself off instead."

He frowned, several emotions flickering across his features. "That's because I wanted to, Carrie. It felt amazing for me. I loved every second. And of course you're not going to be a pro when you've never done it before."

"But I want to be a pro, for you," I croaked, my throat clogged with emotion.

He swallowed hard. "You want to know anything, you let Daddy teach you, okay? You don't go behind my back to chat up other guys."

I dropped my head. "I know, Daddy."

"You don't need to learn from other men. I can teach you

everything you need to know about sex, right here, in this barn or in my bed. You understand?"

I nodded miserably.

"Did you get off on talking to him?"

I shook my head vigorously.

He gave me a hard look. "He sent you a dick pic. Did you like looking at it?"

"No, not at all. I swear. That's when I knew I'd made a mistake."

He was silent for a long time. I hoped he was figuring out that I was telling the truth, but he looked more dismayed than ever.

At last, his gaze trailed between my thighs.

I hated that I was tied up like this. My pussy spread wide, exposed.

He reached out and roughly cupped it with his hand. "Soaking wet," he commented. Then he drew back his hand, and gave it a slap.

I groaned. That actually felt good. It stung, but it was also really pleasurable. He gave me another slap, then another one. When I failed to stifle another sound, he stared into my eyes, his own sapphire irises hot and blazing.

"Oh, you like that, huh?" he said.

I made a noncommittal sound.

"Want me to slap your pussy again?"

"Yes," I whispered.

His lips curled into a thin smile. "Then ask me."

"Please... slap my pussy."

"You sure?" His drawl was slow and cruel. Just what I needed.

"Yes, Daddy. Please. Make it hurt."

He obliged. He slapped me harder than before, alternating between my pussy and my inner thighs so I never knew where the next one was going to land. The ones on my thighs hurt so bad, while the ones on my pussy drove me crazy.

He stood back and looked at me thoughtfully. "I think you're ready for me again," he said, then reached forward and pushed two fingers inside me. I gasped. I wasn't sore anymore. I just wanted him inside me.

"And you're even wetter than before. You think you've been punished enough?"

I nodded vigorously. I couldn't take any more of that crop on my body.

He looked me up and down as if he couldn't decide what to do with me.

Apprehension raced through my veins, making the hairs on my arms stand on end.

He held the crop up horizontally and pressed it against my lips. "Open," he said.

Automatically, I opened my mouth and he pushed it between my lips. It tasted sour and salty, but I didn't dare spit it out.

"Hold it there for me." He unfastened the straps on my wrists and ankles.

"I don't know what to do now," he said. "When I dominate you, it's for your own good. It's not because I don't respect you. It's nothing like the things that happen in porn. I need you to understand that. Now, I want to see you on your hands and knees. Keep that crop right where it is, and give me a turn around the room."

I dropped to the floor. Immediately, my arms burned with pins and needles as the blood rushed back into them, but I ignored the pain as I began to crawl my hands and knees, holding the crop in my teeth.

"Like I taught you," Steele's voice thundered.

Hurriedly, I arched my back, parted my thighs a little more, and tried to keep my posture perfect. My knees were still tender from last time, and the wooden boards were as hard as ever, but I didn't dare complain.

As I went around in a big circle, Steele followed me at a leisurely pace, occasionally slapping my ass to make me go faster. It was as humiliating as hell, but that ache in my pussy grew and grew, and I yearned for him to stop me and plunge his cock into me.

When I approached the hay bale, he patted it.

"Now, get up on here," he told me.

Guessing he wanted me on all fours, I did just that. He took the crop out of my mouth and adjusted my position, spreading my legs a little wider, making me arch my back more, until he was satisfied. He ran his hands all over me again, like a horse dealer examining a potential purchase. Squeezing each breast and thigh, grasping my ass. He ran his hand roughly between my legs, spreading my wetness all the way from my clit to my ass. It was a rough, careless gesture, but I liked it, and I couldn't help rubbing myself against him.

When a moan escaped my lips, he made a sound of irritation.

Abruptly, his finger sank into my asshole. He slid it in and out. It felt weird, but good. Half of me wanted him to stop, the other half hoped he wouldn't. Then something bigger began to enter my ass. Another finger. I groaned. Two of Steele's thick fingers were now inside my most private place. It was too much to take. But when he pumped them in and out, slick with my pussy juices, waves of pleasure spread through my body.

"Are you going to come like that, little one?" he said in a crooning tone.

"No," I mumbled.

"What if that's all I want to give you?"

I mumbled something incomprehensible, unsure what the

right answer was. Distracted by the sensation of his fingers pumping in and out of me.

"What if I only want to fuck your ass? What about those girls in porn who do that all the time?"

I froze as a mixture of horror and excitement took hold of me. I felt dizzy, breathless.

"I want you to take me everywhere, Daddy," I murmured.

Steele drew in a sharp breath. "Really? You want my big cock in your ass?"

"Yes, I do," I said hesitantly, remembering just how big it had felt inside me yesterday. Steele's fingers burned a little as they breached the tight ring of muscle, but it felt good. I liked the hurt. I deserved it.

He kept pumping his fingers in and out of me, kind of casually, but going deeper each time, until I felt his knuckles pressing up against my hole.

"It's going to be deeper than this, and a lot bigger," he told me.

I mumbled something, almost past speech.

Abruptly, he withdrew his fingers from me. "Soon, but not today," he told me. "Today is when I teach you to suck my cock like a pro."

He made me stay in position on the hay bale like it was some kind of podium, my ass and pussy all exposed for him, while he walked around me in a circle.

He stopped in front of me, the fly of his jeans barely capable of containing his erection.

"I was going to save this for later in your training," he told me. "But it's going to be part of the lesson I'm going to teach you for looking at porn." He stood right in front of my face, and slowly unfastened his zipper and pulled out his cock. I quailed at the sight of it. What I'd told him before was true—looking at the men's cocks on the porn videos did nothing for me. They looked gross compared to his. He had a beautiful cock—perfectly shaped, like sculpted marble. But it was just so *big*.

I expected him to bring it to my lips, but instead he told me to open my mouth.

"Wider," he said with impatience.

I did as he told me, and a fresh burst of arousal burned through my body. It felt shameful posing like this, all of me open to him. He slid two fingers into my mouth. "Keep it open," he warned me as he ran his fingertips over my teeth, the inside of my cheeks, and my tongue, gliding right to the back, until I gagged.

He slid his fingers out halfway, then tried again. I gagged again, hard.

"Try harder," he said. "Don't think about what's happening, and breathe deeply through your nose."

I tried again, wanting to do better for him this time. I lasted a little longer.

"Good," he said. "Now, try to take my cock."

He pushed it between my lips, but he was so big, it barely fit into my mouth, never mind my throat. He held my head and moved his hips back and forth, working more of himself into my mouth. I gagged again, but this time, he didn't ease back. He kept going.

"Good girl," he crooned, going deeper and deeper. Almost before I knew it, his cock was going right into my throat.

"Suck Daddy's cock," he murmured, as he pushed in and in and in. "Yeah, that's right." He held me tight, thrusting into me, fucking my mouth. His cock cut off my airway and I had to gulp for air every time he withdrew. I tried not to freak out; tried to focus on doing my best for my daddy, taking more and more of him.

His hips moved faster and faster and he tugged painfully on my hair. All I could do was breathe, and receive him. "You're doing great," he said.

It felt dirty and demeaning and fucking hot to be used like that.

In and out, in and out, he went. Fucking me. Thrusting into my throat, while I was powerless against the relentless rhythm.

At last, he gave a deep sound of satisfaction and came, his hot, salty cum hitting the back of my throat. I swallowed fast, and he kept thrusting, until the last traces of his climax had faded.

"You did good," he told me, stroking my face. I panted, trying to catch my breath. My eyes had teared up and my throat felt raw, but I glowed with satisfaction.

I'd redeemed myself. I felt proud.

But I still had to explain. "I'm sorry, Daddy. I'll never do it again. I was trying to be good. I wanted to be as good as her."

Steele's forehead wrinkled. "Who?"

"Your other girl. The lover you mentioned."

"Oh, babygirl." His huge shoulders relaxed a fraction. "You never have to worry about being good enough. I'm not with her; I'm with you." He lifted me easily in his arms. "Let's go inside," he said.

He carried me indoors, holding me close to protect me from the cold night breeze.

He deposited me on the couch with a blanket, and disappeared into the bathroom. I heard the taps running into the tub and gave a sigh of relief. I'd been worried that he was preparing some new punishment for me.

"Bath's ready," he called after a few minutes. I left the blanket behind and walked in.

Steele was crouching beside the tub, his sleeves rolled up and his arm in the water, swishing it around. The water was full of bubbles and it smelled delicious—like pineapples.

He turned his head to look at me. "You like bubble baths?"

I nodded eagerly. I used to, when I was a small child, anyway. He reached for me and helped me step in.

"Temperature okay?" he asked.

"Perfect," I sighed, and slid under the water. It was nice and deep, covering all of me when I lay back. I let my eyelids fall shut, a feeling of comfort washing over me. When I opened them again, Steele was looking at me tenderly.

"How are you feeling, little one?"

"Good," I said.

His forehead furrowed. "It wasn't too much for you tonight, was it?"

I shook my head. "No, it wasn't."

He reached for my hand under the water and squeezed it. "You know your safeword. Don't ever be afraid to use it if things are too much; if I push you beyond your boundaries. Of course..." he ran a finger from my collarbone to my nipple, and tweaked it teasingly, "it's good to test your boundaries. Sometimes you might surprise yourself about the kinds of things you enjoy. But I think you will know in your heart, if anything isn't right for you."

I told him that nothing had been too much. That I felt satisfied and safe.

He looked pleased; relieved, even. "Okay, good. I'm going to keep checking in on you like this. It's called aftercare, and it's an important part of your training. It's where a daddy and his girl check in with each other to make sure they're both okay with what's happened."

I nodded. "I'm okay," I said in a small voice. It was hard thing to admit to. But it was true—screwed up though it might be, I'd enjoyed every bit of it.

"Now, sit forward," he told me. He took a sponge and began to wash me all over, from head to toe. I was so lulled by the experience, so drowsy in the warm water, that I started playing with the bubbles, like I used to when I was a small child—clapping them between my hands, so they burst everywhere.

Suddenly, I froze. "Oops, I didn't mean to do that," I blurted out, prickling with shame.

But a look of tenderness came over Steele's face. "I love to see you playing like this," he said. Then he broke into a grin as he grabbed a handful of bubbles and dumped them right on my head.

I gave a shriek of delight, scooped up a big handful of bubbles, and splashed them onto him.

He yelled out in mock outrage, and retaliated.

It was a foam war, with tidal waves of water splashing everywhere. Soon, we were both drenched in sweet-smelling bubbles.

Steele laughed, wiping his face with a hand towel. I'd never seen him looking so light, so carefree, and it made my tummy feel lovely and warm. "I'm drenched," he exclaimed, examining his wet shirt and jeans, but he didn't look mad about it.

He told me to stand up, took the shower head, and rinsed me off. Then he took a fresh towel out of the airing cupboard and carefully dried me. All the while, a smile played on his lips, like he was enjoying tending to me like that.

I loved it, too. Loved the feeling of relaxing, knowing someone else was taking care of my needs.

Steele wrapped the towel around me and lifted me out of the tub, then he shucked off his wet clothes and climbed in. I stood, feasting my eyes as he soaped up his naked body, his hands running all over his muscular bulk. He was such a vision of manly perfection, from his big pecs, to his tight buns, to his long, clean cock. My arousal had died down while I was in the bath, but now it grew again, into a deep, throbbing need for him. I longed to run my hands all over his sexy body, to caress every single contour and muscle.

He noticed me looking, and flashed a dirty smile. I blushed, embarrassed that my desire for him was so obvious.

We went through to the bedroom, and he took my towel back to the bathroom while I slipped into bed.

When he returned, his cock was semi-hard and my desire went into overdrive. I'd wondered whether he was planning to fuck me or not, and now I was in no doubt.

He slid between the sheets and arched over me, his big body spreading my thighs. I wrapped my legs around him, and we kissed deep and long.

When he reached between my legs and discovered how wet I was, he gave a low growl. He reached into the night-stand drawer for a condom, rolled it on, and in seconds, he was entering me.

It was different from last time—none of the burning as he broke through my maidenhead. Just a big push as his thick cock opened me up, then a blissful, shivery feeling as my muscles yielded to him and he slid all the way home.

I clung to his back as he began to move in me, wanting him close, wanting him to crush me with his big body.

He felt so good inside me, each thrust deep, powerful. Possessing me. Pleasuring me. I loved the way he held my gaze, his emotions showing on his face.

My breathing got heavier until I was panting, whispering his name with every thrust.

Soon, I could feel a climax approaching. I arched my back and held him tighter, longing to come with him inside me like that.

But he pulled out and flipped me over. He slid a pillow under my hips, raising my ass in the air, then entered me from behind. I cried out at this new sensation—as his cock went deep inside.

He started to thrust fast, roughly, his nails digging into my hips and his pelvis butting my ass. It felt intense like this, almost too much to take, and wild animal sounds escaped my lips.

Faster and faster he went, until I came hard, crying out, my face buried in the pillow.

He wasn't done yet. He pulled me over, onto my side, and held me in his arms, spooning me. Now his hands roamed over my breasts and clit, and I wriggled around, onto my side, so we could kiss at the same time.

Steele kept changing positions—putting me on my back, front, side, legs up against my chest—each one pleasuring me in a different way. I felt like a ragdoll, helpless to the orgasms he drew from me, one after the other, after the other.

Finally, when I was exhausted, both of us damp with perspiration, Steele laid me on my back again, and looked right into my eyes as he came.

It was beautiful to see the way his irises went dark, to see pure bliss transforming his features. He pulled out of me fast, but stayed right there, kissing me for a long, long time, and I felt so happy and overwhelmed that my eyes teared up.

CHAPTER 15

Carrie

*F*or the next couple of days, there were no more punishments. Steele seemed kind of different. I didn't have a name for it exactly, but there was a new softness in the way he look at me.

We just worked, and did regular things together. We went to the supermarket and stocked up on a ton of food. It was kind of fun choosing things. Steele confessed that he used to hate shopping. He'd stock up for a month at a time, have a day when he made a big batch of stew, then he'd put it in the freezer and eat it almost every day. But now, we planned meals together. He was passionate about eating healthy—no junk food. Everything had to be fresh: meat, vegetables and potatoes.

Although, he said that if I was a good girl, when we were done shopping, I could choose one tub of ice cream. I picked chocolate and caramel because I knew chocolate was his favorite, and a little caramel might help broaden his horizons.

He also bought me a new sim card for my phone, and put me on a plan. I was connected to the world again.

"You'd better not tell anyone where you are, though—at least for a while," he said.

A thread of nerves prickled inside me, as it always did when I thought of my life back in Texas. "But you haven't found anything on the news?"

"No, I haven't. But let's be cautious," he told me, squeezing my hand.

I nodded. It had been three weeks since I'd stabbed Enzo. Steele kept assuring me that everything was fine; if he'd died, we'd know about it by now. But I couldn't stop worrying. I wished I could call up someone from home and find out for sure, but that would be madness.

No, I'd just have to keep this on my conscience. In the meantime, Steele did everything he could to help me forget about it.

I installed some apps on my phone, but stayed off Instagram and Facebook. I wasn't even sure I wanted to get in touch with people from my old life. I missed a couple of my girlfriends. I'd message them one day to let them know I was okay. But everything from my past was like a dream, already fading so fast, while my life here was in high definition. One beautiful day after another, full of new experiences and exciting feelings.

* * *

When the weekend came, we still had to wake up early and take care of the animals, of course, but we didn't do any other work. Instead, Steele took me for a drive along the river to see the fall colors. The water sparkled so prettily as it meandered through the valley, and the trees burned beautiful shades of red and orange. He told me all about the land, about its ancestral people. And I could tell he loved it, and that it was a deep part of him and his soul. I started to love it, too, because I wanted to be part of him—and him part of me, too.

I was falling for Steele. But was he falling for me, too? Did him being my daddy mean he'd fallen for me already? It was confusing. He said he was going to be my daddy forever, but did that mean he loved me? More than anything, I longed to ask him. But there was a little part of me that was worried he'd laugh at me. That he'd tell me that wasn't how things worked.

* * *

THAT NIGHT, Steele took me out to dinner again—to the same place where we'd met Barbara and Tom. He said it would just be the two of us this time, even if every single friend of his was in there. My heart fluttered in delight. He always put me first, always cared for my happiness.

He'd reserved the best table again, by the window, and as the candlelight flickered and he held my hand across the table, I felt like the luckiest girl in the world. It was a perfect, romantic evening. I was wearing the pink dress again. Steele said I looked prettier than ever. But he'd have to get me some more outfits for dates.

"We'll go to the city in a couple of weeks," he said. "There's nothing special enough for you in the local department store." Then he frowned, because I didn't say anything. "Would you like that?" he asked, an endearing touch of uncertainty in his voice.

I clasped my hands together. "Yes, I would love that," I said. "But who's going to take care of the animals?"

He laughed. "You're already turning into a country girl. I'll ask one of the neighbors. That's what we do around here —take turns helping each other out. It's a real community."

"I can tell," I said happily, and we started making plans to drive to Vancouver. He said we could stay somewhere fancy if I wanted, and we could go to bars, restaurants, whatever I liked. Shop all day if I wanted.

"I just want to spend time with you," I told him, and he looked pleased.

He raised my hand and pressed it to his lips. "I want you to be happy and have fun, little one. I don't want to deprive you of anything."

"Oh, everything I want is right here," I assured him, my eyes prickling with unshed tears.

"Good, baby. I'm glad." He hesitated before saying, "My last submissive preferred the city to the country. But she didn't tell me straight. She came to live with me anyway, even though she was unhappy. I thought I was the one making her miserable. I didn't realize she was lying to me, that we just weren't compatible because we wanted different things. Maybe she was lying to herself." He added the last part thoughtfully.

I squeezed his hand. "I like the country. I'm not lying."

"I know you're not, babygirl. You're a terrible liar."

I stuck my tongue out at him, and he chuckled. "Careful." The warning made me smile.

By the time the food came to our fancy table, I was more relaxed. It was nice to know I fit Daddy better than his last lady love. I'd been mentally trying to measure up to her, without knowing anything about her. An impossible task.

The starter and entrée were as delicious as last time, and

it when it came to desserts, Steele looked at the list earnestly. "I'm guessing you'll be ordering the ice cream medley with a side of caramel sauce?" he said. It was at the bottom of the list, as a suggestion for little ones.

I nodded, my cheeks warming. "Guess I will."

Steele broke into a grin. He liked treating me like a lady, but I knew he really loved it when I was his little one.

When we got back to the ranch, Steele took me to bed and made love to me. I was learning there were two sides to our sex life. One was the rough, wild fucking that accompanied training in the barn. I loved it; I loved the way I could feel so unrestrained that I didn't care what screams and cries came out of my mouth. How desperate and helpless I felt. How Steele unraveled me, laid me bare, and taught me things about myself that I'd never even considered before.

And then there was the lovemaking in bed, which was full of tenderness. Steele looked into my eyes, and murmured sweet words to me. His hands caressed me gently and he went down on me for hours, drawing one orgasm after another from my helpless body.

When he had given me all the orgasms I could stand, something in him would shift, and he'd fuck me hard as hard as he needed to, before he came deep inside me. In these moments I felt the barely-contained fire inside him. Sensed how much it cost him to hold back.

Tonight, he lay on his back and pulled me on top of him. As I sat back, with all my weight on him, his cock pushed deep inside me. I couldn't believe I could fit it all in. He held my hands by my thighs and looked up at me adoringly. "They call this the cowgirl position, you know?" he said.

I grinned. "They do?"

"Ride me, baby," he murmured. "I want to see your sweet pussy sliding up and down my cock."

Steele liked to watch. He switched on the lamps on the nightstands, and his gaze fluttered over me as we made love. He loved to see his cock possessing my body, over and over again.

He was still big for me, but I learned to accommodate him. Learned to love the fleeting shock as he penetrated me, knowing it would soon give way to intense ripples of pleasure.

I leaned back, as he wanted me to, and he held onto my hips, lifting me up and down on his cock.

"You look so sexy," he said. It turned me on that he could see my pussy filled with his big cock. I was learning that I was a bit of an exhibitionist.

Soon, he pulled me close so I was lying flat on top of him. He held me tight and thrust into me, all the while kissing me deeply. His tongue slipped into my mouth while his cock filled me right up. As his rhythm matched my own, I could feel a climax approaching, coming closer and closer and closer. But he didn't let me go—he kept kissing me, so when the orgasm hit, I cried out right into his mouth. It was deep and intense and beautiful.

"I love you," he murmured.

I went very still. "What did you say?"

"I said I love you, Carrie."

I blinked. "You said you love me?"

He grinned. "Yes, of course I do. Why the surprise?"

I shook my head. "I don't know. I-I love you too," I stuttered as my eyes filled with tears.

"Oh, baby." He held my head in his hands and kissed the tears away. "Of course I do. I should've told you already."

I laid my head down on his chest and he hugged me tight, his cock still deep inside me. When he started to thrust again, fast and rough, I was on the point of coming again, and for the first time, we came at the same time in a dazzling kalei-doscope of bliss.

I couldn't quit smiling.

My daddy had said he loved me. It was the one little piece that had been missing, and now it slotted right into place.

CHAPTER 16

Carrie

After that night, our relationship seemed to enter a deeper level. I sensed Steele felt it, too. He was more relaxed around me. Sure, he was still a stickler for discipline, and I understood that was always going to be a part of our relationship. And secretly, I was glad. His hand on my bottom brought me peace, helped push away the past, and drew me fully into my new life, where I knew what the rules were. Where I knew, without a shred of doubt, that I had a daddy who would take care of me and give me all the guidance I needed. He told me I still needed a lot of training. I was only half broken, he said, his eyes crinkling at the corners. He sometimes wondered if I'd ever be fully broken.

Sometimes, I got bratty and he sensed I needed a spanking. "Come here," he'd tell me, out of nowhere, "and lie across my lap."

I'd do as he told me, of course, stretching out, positioning my ass across his muscular thighs, half worrying, half yearning for him to take down my jeans and my panties, and lay his hand on my bare cheeks. First, the spanking, until my ass was red and sore, and then the sex—always the sex. Because by the time he'd finished spanking me, my pussy would be wet enough to leave a mark on his jeans, while his cock was so hard it was bursting out of his pants.

The training in the barn continued, too. He started to let me ride Megan, and that was our routine—a lesson on Megan, then a lesson with me stripped naked in the barn. I understood the two things were related. He always found some fault in my posture, with the aids I was giving the little horse. And when we got to the barn and he made me strip, he always used those as the basis to correct me.

He made me a collar out of an old horse rein. It was brown leather and well-worn. He attached a buckle to the end of it, and at the start of our training sessions, he fastened it around my neck. "Now you'll know that your training is beginning," he told me. "That you need to perform for me, exactly as I tell you." He ran his hands over my body—my breasts, ass, pussy—reminding me that I was his, to discipline, train, and possess.

I did my best to go through my paces, doing laps around the room on my hands and knees, ass high, back arched. But more often than not, he'd take the crop to me, striping my ass and thighs, until he was satisfied with my performance.

He liked to position me on the hay bale and walk around me in circles as if I was an art exhibit. He'd take his big cock out of his pants and run his hand up and down his shaft thoughtfully, as if deciding how he was going to fuck me next. I would pose for him, quivering in anticipation. Whether he decided to take my mouth or my pussy, I knew I was going to enjoy it. He hadn't taken my ass yet, but he teased it a lot, and every day I longed for it a little more.

One day, Steele made me take my position on the hay bale. Head and ass lifted high, all wet and exposed for him. He'd been quiet this morning, as if turning something over in his mind.

He got the crop and trailed it over my body, finishing with some sharp taps on my pussy. Then he went and stood behind me, long enough for me to fidget and shift my position. But I knew better than to ask him questions. Instead, I waited silently, apprehension tingling in my veins. Was he planning to spank me? To fuck me?

Instead, he told me to kneel up.

He tapped my inner thighs with the crop, easing my knees apart until they were wide enough for his satisfaction, exposing my bare pussy to him.

"Now, put your hands behind your back."

I did as he said, and he went behind me and bound my wrists together with something—one of his leather straps, no doubt. He'd never done this before. It made me feel hot and vulnerable. My back was arched and my breasts were thrust out.

He stood in front of me, admiring his handiwork. "I want you to stay right there and not move until I get back, understood?"

I nodded.

"If you move an inch, I will know, and you will not enjoy the punishment."

I nodded again, acknowledging his words. He took something out of his back pocket—a handkerchief. He tied it around my eyes, and the world went black.

A dart of nerves shot through me. He'd never blindfolded me before, either. I wasn't sure if I liked it or not. It made me feel hella vulnerable.

He was gone a long time. Enough time for my wetness to chill on my spread pussy. Enough times for me to wonder if he was ever coming back. Anticipation gave way to boredom, and returned to anticipation again. *What is he doing?*

My knees started to ache. I tried hard not to fidget.

At long last, I heard footsteps on the wooden boards of the barn. The blindfold was pulled off my eyes, and Steele stood in front of me, holding a medium-sized cardboard box, his eyes lit with suppressed excitement.

It was the package that had arrived yesterday, I recalled. Steele had brought it inside and hidden it somewhere. I'd longed to ask what it was, but sensed I might regret the question.

Now, he sat down on the end of the hay bale and opened it up. There was a bunch of brown leather straps, with brass rings connecting them. Not the old leather of his horse tack, but shiny new leather, with a rich, expensive scent.

He held the straps up to show me. "Know what it is?"

"A... a harness?" I muttered, confused.

He smiled, pleased. "It's for you to wear as part of your training," he told me. He untied my hands and helped me to my feet.

There were two sets of straps to step into, and then he pulled the harness up, over my body, tightening various buckles around my waist, ribcage, and shoulders.

He stepped back and admired his handiwork. "Beautiful," he said in a tone of satisfaction. "Want to see how you look?"

I nodded uncertainly.

He grabbed his phone from his pocket, snapped a photo, and showed it to me.

My breath caught. It *was* beautiful, really. Kind of like a one-piece bathing suit, made of expensive, intricately finished leather. My body was tightly encased in a series of straps, leaving my breasts and pussy bare.

"Well, what do you think?" There was the slightest hint of uncertainty in his voice.

"I like it," I said. It was arousing to be so tightly constricted, yet exposed at the same time. I felt like some kind of expensive, highly-prized creature. A thoroughbred horse.

Steele ran his hands over me and I could tell he enjoyed the combination of skin and leather.

"Lovely," he murmured, with a catch in his voice. He pinched my nipples hard and slapped my pussy. "From now on, you'll wear the harness when I put you through your paces. And if I think you need it, I might make you wear it in the house as well."

A dart of arousal went through me, so sharp it hurt.

"Now I've got one more thing to give you, but you need to be on your hands and knees to receive it." He nodded at the hay bale.

Immediately I climbed onto it, getting into position automatically—ass high, thighs wide apart. He removed the final item from the box almost reverently.

I frowned. It was a coil of blonde hair. When he held it aloft, it tumbled down into a ponytail, bright and silken. Something was attached to the end of it—a transparent bulb.

"Know what it is?" he asked me.

I stared at the bulb, recognition beginning to dawn on me. "Is it for my ass?" I asked.

"Yup. It's a butt plug. It's going to train your ass, while I train the rest of you."

He disappeared behind me, and I started to tremble. I'd heard of butt plugs. But they'd always seemed like kind of a joke. I couldn't imagine what it would be like to have one in my ass.

The plug brushed against my pussy, and I fought the urge to jerk away, knowing what the consequences would be.

"Steady," Steele said soothingly, and he stroked my ass cheeks as he often did when I was nervous. He rubbed the bulb up and down my labia. It felt soft and arousing. Then he pushed it into my pussy. I took it easily. It didn't feel so big—there, anyway.

"I'm just going to make it nice and wet for you," he commented.

I *was* wet—wetter than ever. As much as the thought of the butt plug scared my conscious mind, my subconscious seemed to be eager for it.

He took it out and pressed it against my little hole. It started to go in so easily, I almost didn't feel it. But it quickly got wider and wider, until it was really big. I could feel it forcing me open, my muscles yielding to accept it. It started to hurt, and I cried out in a panic.

Then there was a little pop, and it didn't feel so big anymore.

"There," Steele said, and he stepped in front of me again.

I had a second of confusion. *He's left the butt plug inside me?* My ass felt really full but open at the same time, and my pussy burned with a fresh surge of arousal.

"How does it feel?" he asked.

"Weird. Hot," I admitted.

"Well, you look beautiful. Like a perfect little pony girl," he told me.

He took another photo and showed me. There I was in a horse harness, with a blonde tail—the exact same color as the hair on my head—hanging down from my behind. I felt the hairs brushing against my pussy, and squirmed. It was a weird, humiliating feeling, but all the more hot for that.

Steele put me through my paces again: walking turns around the barn, first on two legs, and then on my hands and knees. The brass rings clinked, and the leather straps chafed a little at the tops of my thighs, and the tail swished, but that was nothing compared to the sensation of the butt plug in my ass—stretching me open, driving me crazy. I could feel my wetness running down my thighs, and my cheeks burned at the thought that Steele could see it, too, and he knew how much this shameful game was turning me on.

When I'd completed enough laps to Steele's satisfaction, he told me to get back on the hay bale again. He stood behind me, and I heard the clink as he unfastened his belt, the sound of his zipper being undone, then the soft plop of his jeans and underwear falling to the floor. I liked it when he stripped like this, keeping his cowboy shirt on. It was kind of functional and dirty.

I began to shiver in anticipation, unsure what he was planning next. I heard a rustle of foil, a quiet snap of rubber, and something pressed at my entrance. A moment later, he was pushing himself inside me.

He was going to fuck me with the butt plug still in my ass.

Holy crap, this felt different. The butt plug took up so much space, there was hardly any room for his cock. He pushed harder than usual, until he hit home with a groan of pleasure.

I gasped. I was stuffed. Both my holes were filled up. It was too much.

My insides throbbed and spasmed.

He hadn't thrust three times before I exploded. An insane, shattering orgasm. It shuddered through my pussy and my ass at the same time. I dropped my head into my hands and gave myself over to it, aware of nothing but the brutal, beautiful sensations.

"*God*, you feel so good, baby," Steele murmured as he thrust into me again and again. "So tight." I could feel his hand on the end of the butt plug, holding the naughty ponytail out of the way as he fucked my pussy. It was rough and dirty and animalistic. He tugged on the straps that encircled my hips, fucking me harder and harder. Wild, jerky, out of control. Slamming into me again and again....

Until, at last, he came with a deep, animal sound of release.

When he pulled the butt plug out, slowly, slowly, I was relieved. But I also knew I'd look forward to the next time he used it to train my ass.

CHAPTER 17

Steele

I trained her every day—my little pony girl. I couldn't get enough of the sight of her in her harness. The elegant leather displayed her sweet body to perfection. I was so proud of her. So proud of the way she tried her hardest to please me; obeyed all my orders.

And the training was doing wonders for her. Her posture was transformed. Even in the house, she walked tall and confident. That teenage slouch of hers was completely gone.

I made her take the plug all the time, and she never complained. The sight of the swishy blonde tail hanging down between her legs, brushing her pussy, almost drove me to distraction. It meant trust, and submission.

And it made her soaking wet and desperate for me to take her. Often, I claimed her from behind while she was on her knees on the hay bale, or bent over the couch. I loved how tight it made her pussy, the wild sounds that burst from her lips when she came.

Other times, I liked to pull it out first, and gaze at her sweet asshole while I fucked her, knowing I was going to claim it soon as well.

I knew she was scared of taking my cock there; scared it was going to break her in two.

I was patient, for the most part. Whenever I spanked her —which was most days—and she was lying across my knee, jeans and panties down by her ankles, and her cheeks bright red, I'd finish by training her ass. Sometimes I'd use my fingers, adding one at a time, sliding them in and out, while my other hand teased her clit. Sometimes, I'd use the plug, pushing it in to its widest part, then withdrawing it again. I wouldn't quit until she came, and when I watched her exploding in an intense orgasm, I'd feel her little hole spasming as well.

But whenever my cock nudged against her opening instead, she tensed right up.

There was no rush, I told her. And, aside from my need to possess every part of her, there wasn't. It would happen when it happened.

One beautiful day passed after another, in loving, companionable days and hot, lustful nights. The first snow came, bringing peace and silence across the land. Carrie was as excited as a small child. She insisted on making her first ever snowman in the yard in front of the house, then she expanded it into a whole snow family—mom, dad and two kids. I loved to see her so joyous and unaffected—just as she was supposed to be. The sight of her working with rosy cheeks and a big grin on her face touched my heart.

Max had quit bothering me about the ranch when I told him he could have his half if he came and took over my job for the winter. I was calling his bluff, and it worked. He told me he'd be staying in the city for the duration.

So it was just Carrie and me, and the animals, cozy in our winter wonderland.

I allowed myself to start daydreaming. To picture our future together. In my imagination, it was always a riot of color and intensity, as broad and infinite as the plains. I imagined children—not for a long time, of course. Carrie had plenty of growing up to do first. But, in time, maybe two girls and two boys. I'd expand the ranch, maybe build a whole new house for them. Teach them to ride before they were big enough to walk.

But for now, and for a long time, I wanted it to be just me and Carrie, loving each other, deepening our bond every day. It was a happiness I'd never imagined.

Until one day in late November, when everything changed.

* * *

I WAS FIXING a broken fence in the farthest field of the ranch when I spotted something in my peripheral vision—a small figure, moving in the distance. I stood up to see better. It was Carrie, hurtling toward me at full pelt.

Something was wrong. I started running, too, my heart jumping into my throat.

I caught up to her in the middle of the next field. She looked panicked, tears running down her face.

"He's found me!" she wailed.

"Who?"

She held out her phone with a trembling hand, and I snatched it. As I read the words on the screen, a furious rage surged in me:

Where the fuck are you little puta?

You better get your ass back here Carrie!

I mean it. come home now

Last chance if you don't come back now I'm telling the cops what really happened

"That goddarned piece of dung." I clenched the phone so hard, the plastic crackled.

"I'm going to have to go back, aren't I?" Carrie choked out. She was sobbing now, almost hysterical.

"What? No." I dropped to my knees in the snow and wrapped my arms around her. She felt tiny, her chest heaving like a little bird's. I pushed her hair out of her face and made her look at me. "Listen, Carrie, there is no way you're going back home. Are you crazy?"

She wiped her nose on her sleeve. "B-but, he's going to tell the cops. And I'll go to jail."

I shook my head. "He's bluffing. If he tells the cops you stabbed him, he'll have to tell them why."

"But he'll say I'm lying. There's no proof of what he did to me. Tried to do, anyway."

I exhaled slowly, pushing my anger away so I could concentrate on her. "Carrie, I'm here to protect you. You have to know I'll do that with my last breath."

Her lip trembled. "I know you will. But I don't want you to get in trouble, either."

"Hold up. Let's see what kind of state he's in." I took my own phone out of my pocket and refreshed the search I'd done so many times before. I actually hadn't trawled the news for a few days, thinking it had been long enough.

That had been a mistake.

There he was. I ground my teeth.

Enzo Gutierrez hailed a hero after tackling a burglar. Released from hospital today.

said the Lone Star News article. It went on to explain that he'd sustained a serious knife wound when confronting an intruder. He'd endured six hours of surgery, and barely escaped with his life.

Pride was my first reaction—for what my little one had done. A little messed up, but there it was. I was relieved that piece of crap wasn't dead, for Carrie's sake, but it looked like she'd put him in the hospital for a month. Maybe he'd think twice about taking advantage of vulnerable women again.

"Let me see?" Carrie demanded. I handed her my phone, and her eyes got bigger and bigger. "He's okay," she said.

"A lot more than he deserves." I stared at the photo of the 'hero's' homecoming in disgust. He looked about as slimy and weaselly as I'd expected.

Carrie's phone pinged again. She glanced at it and gasped. Her face turned pale.

"Let me see."

As I read the words on the screen, my sympathy for Carrie overflowed:

Carrie honey, you have to come back. Enzo told me what you did and I forgive you. But if you don't come back, he's gonna be real mad. Please baby, I need you.

"Your mom, I presume?"

Carrie's lip curled. "If you can call her that." A look of sheer disgust crossed her face. But then she fell apart.

I took her in my arms again. "Oh, baby, I'm so sorry," I muttered as she sobbed. My throat felt tight and my heart ached for everything she must have endured growing up.

"I have to go back, don't I?" she whimpered. "When your mom asks, you go."

I drew back, and grasped her shoulders. "No, you don't. Not when your own parent willingly exposes you to danger. Carrie, listen to me: I know you're loyal to your mom, but nothing good will come of going back to Texas. All that will happen is you'll get hurt."

She bit down on her lip, which was already red and chewed. "I know."

"You're here now, with me. And I'm going to protect you, okay?"

She gazed at me wordlessly for a while.

"Okay," she said at last. But there was conflict in those big green eyes of hers, and it worried me.

* * *

EVERY TIME I thought of Carrie's mother, my skull started to pound. *Manipulating her own daughter like that? Allowing her to be abused?* I couldn't wrap my head around it. Enzo was human garbage, that was obvious. *But her mom's own flesh and blood?*

A child's bond with its parent is strong, no matter how little the parent deserves it—I understood that. But I thought I'd managed to persuade Carrie that going back home was a terrible idea.

That evening, I lit a fire and we sat on the couch under a blanket. I snuggled Carrie in my arms, encouraging her until, haltingly, she told me more about her childhood.

"When I was twelve or something," she said, her voice no more than a whisper, "my mom used to get her boyfriend to babysit me while she was at work. 'Keep your hands to your-self, Ron!' she'd say before she left. Because she knew. She knew he was a perv, and so did I. I was so scared of being alone with him, I used to climb out my bedroom window and wait in the yard till she got back.

"And this other guy—he used to show me dirty photos on his phone. My mom used to tell him to quit, but she never actually stopped him. She acted like he was just being a pain in the butt, kidding around, but those photos really freaked me out. They were like, full on. Girls being hurt and stuff."

With every story, I got more and more sickened, and my admiration for my little wild girl grew. I knew she'd been through a lot, but this was off the scale. It was a miracle she still had her pure heart, and was capable of trust.

"I'm surprised you trusted me so easily," I said, thinking aloud.

She regarded me seriously. "You're different, Steele. Nothing like those guys. Believe me."

Suddenly she looked wise—a lot older than her years.

I lifted her hand and kissed it. "I'll never betray your trust," I told her. I saw in her eyes that she believed me.

But it wasn't enough.

Steele

*N*ext morning, when I opened my eyes, Carrie was standing at the foot of the bed, peering into the closet.

"What are you doing, baby?" I muttered, not really awake yet.

She turned around, and I saw with a lurch of dismay that her face was wet with tears.

"Hey, come here." I threw the covers back and opened my arms. She ran into them, sobbing. "What's going on?" I muttered into her hair.

"Steele, I'm so, so sorry, but I've got to go." She was crying so hard, she could barely get the words out.

My gut tightened. "You mean go back to Texas? Carrie, we talked about this already. You can't."

She snuffled loudly. "I got another message from my

mom." She pulled her phone out of her back pocket and showed me the screen:

Carrie, I need you to come take care of Destiny for a while. There's no one else.

I frowned. "Who's Destiny?"

"My baby cousin." Carrie swallowed hard. "The daughter of my mom's sister. Who is just as screwed up as she is. She's left Destiny with us a few times when she's been in rehab or whatever."

A sickening feeling began to creep through my veins. "How old is Destiny?" I asked.

"Twelve." Carrie lifted her head and met my gaze. "She's pretty, too."

She didn't have to spell it out. An even younger girl around Enzo? That was bad news.

I worked my jaw back and forth. "We can find a solution. Speak to child services."

But she shook her head. "Things don't work like that in the real world. They won't do anything. I have to go back, Steele. I have to move back home and make sure Destiny's okay. Like Mom says, there's no one else."

"Carrie, no. You're not going back. You can't put yourself in danger while trying to help your cousin out. You know that, don't you?" My voice was loud, and she flinched.

"I have to!" she shouted back.

"But he'll hurt you, too. I can't allow this."

Her face twisted. "I don't have a choice. Don't you get that?"

"You do have a choice. I'm telling you that. And you should trust me, because I'm your daddy. You should trust that I know what's best for you."

"I do believe you know what's best for *me*," she said. "B-but I need to think about Destiny, and my useless mom as well." She tried to laugh, but it came out as a hiccup. "This isn't real, Steele. It's a game we're playing, and… well, it's time to enter the real world again."

My veins filled with molten lead. "Carrie, listen to me. You're not thinking straight. You're putting yourself in a dangerous situation, and that's no way of protecting your cousin. I forbid you from going back there. We'll figure something else out." My voice rang out in the small room, and she shrank away from me.

"I have a responsibility," she said quietly, and her eyes were so full of sadness, it cut me. "It's where I belong. These are my people. I need to make sure Destiny is safe—I need to keep her away from Enzo. And the only way I can do that is by being there."

"What if her mom never collects her, Carrie? You can't put your life on hold like that."

She took a deep, shuddering breath. "Steele, the decision has been made for me. It was made for me at birth. I'm not good enough for you. I've always known that, but I've tried not to think about it. You deserve someone who is your equal, your match in all things. Not some poor white trash little girl, with a fucked up family."

All the air went out of me, and I couldn't speak for a while. "Carrie you're not trash. Far from it. You're the most amazing person I can imagine. And you are my equal. You complement me in every way, and we're so happy together. At least, I thought we were."

She nodded miserably. "I was very happy, too. But I can't be happy knowing that Enzo has this power over my mom and Destiny. They're not strong. So I need to go back and be strong for them."

"And if I tell you that you can't?"

She was silent for a while, her chest rising and falling. "I'm sorry, I have to."

I ground my jaw back and forth. "This thing we've had going on between us. It meant nothing to you, did it?"

She gazed at me, and fresh tears ran down her face. "It means everything. I've loved being your little one."

"But not enough to trust me to be your daddy forever. The minute it gets hard, you cut and run."

"It's not like that—" She broke off and clapped a hand over her mouth as she choked up with sobs again. "Steele, this is the worst decision I've ever had to make my life. These weeks I spent with you have been the happiest—maybe even the only happy—time of my entire life. But I have to go back and deal with this. I have responsibilities. Being here with you has always been like the most beautiful dream. You're every girl's fantasy." She reached out and touched my thigh. "The best guy imaginable. But all of this—this ugliness—well, it's a part of me. I've got to go and face it."

"How will you get back?"

She exhaled hard. "I've got a passport."

I shook my head. "What?"

"We were supposed to visit Enzo's family in Mexico at one point, so we all got passports."

I frowned. "But you didn't use it to cross the border?"

"'Course not. Didn't want them to track me here."

I scanned her face in the dim light of the bedroom. "You've made your mind up, haven't you?"

"I have," she said, her voice no more than a whisper. "I'm so sorry. After all you've done for me... Maybe one day, I can come back—"

"Sure," I snapped. A furious torrent of anger poured through me. I pushed her away from me, grabbed the clothes I'd left hanging over a chair, and stormed out of the room, no longer able to contain the emotions welling up inside me.

I'd thought it was bad when Victoria left. But this was so much worse. I felt like my sternum was being ripped wide open, and my heart was being torn out. I was in love with my little one, and she was leaving me. My whole world was crashing down on my head.

I charged out of the house, snatched up a saddle and bridle from the tack room, and strode over to the stables. My thoughts crackled in my head like an electrical storm—hectic and unpredictable. I barely felt in control of my own body.

When I opened the door to Rex's stall, he was calm. He'd gotten used to me. I'd made good progress with his training lately, and had even gotten him to accept the saddle on his back. Next session, I'd been planning to throw my weight over him, too. But now, when I slipped the rope bridle over his head, led him out of the stall, and fastened the saddle over his back, I mounted him.

Right away, he reared up with a squeal of surprise. But I clung on. He reared and bucked and screamed, trying everything to get me off. But I kicked him in the ribs and rode on out of the yard. He was barely ready for riding yet. It was madness. But right now, I didn't care about anything.

He bolted for the wide open plains, and I clung tight, wanting to obliterate every single thing in the world.

* * *

Carrie

I RUSHED out the house after Steele. But it was too late, he'd already gone. And Rex's stall was empty. Steele had ridden off on that crazy horse! I started to run after him, across the fields, but it was madness. They were galloping full pelt, already a speck in the distance.

I returned to the yard and sat on the steps, staring at the

spot where Steele had disappeared from view, terror clutching at every muscle in my body.

He shouldn't be riding Rex. He knew the horse wasn't ready. And he was only doing it because of me. My heart was breaking. I thought I'd cried myself out, but I discovered I had more tears. Steele hated me now, and I didn't blame him. We'd said *forever* to each other, and now I was leaving.

Going back to Texas was the dead last thing I wanted to do. The thought of seeing Enzo again—full of vengeance— made me sick to my stomach. And my mom—I knew I had to take care of her. She couldn't help that she was weak and had never learned good morals. But right now, I hated her so bad. I knew she was using Destiny to get at me. And it was working. There was no way I could refuse to take care of my baby cousin. I had to keep her safe from Enzo.

All this happiness. All this love here with Steele. It already felt like a beautiful dream, fading away.

I'd never really believed Steele and I would last, never believed I deserved a guy like him. And the fact was, I didn't. Because my background was a part of me.

Steele was so, so mad at me. This was nothing like when I did something bad and he punished me. The hurt in his eyes had destroyed me. I wanted to take it all back. Take back every hurtful word. Toss my phone away, and forget about everything except for Steele and me, and our beautiful life together.

He'd never forgive me for this, and I didn't blame him. He'd promised me the world, and I was rejecting it in favor of my miserable trashy life in Texas. That fucking Enzo. For the first time, I wished I really had killed him. It would have saved my mom and Destiny, and maybe I could have spent the rest of my life hiding out here with Steele.

No. That was crazy. Because that would have meant Steele would be guilty of aiding and abetting a fugitive. I had to go back and face my own destiny. I got up and paced around the yard, worriedly. Steele had been gone at least an hour. I was so terrified for him on his crazy horse.

I didn't know what to do. Part of me thought it would be better if I just grabbed my stuff and left before he got back. But I'd be walking, and he'd catch up to me, and I couldn't leave until I knew he was safe.

I forced myself to get started on the chores. No reason to leave the horses in their own mess because my world was falling apart.

I was halfway through cleaning out Moonshine's stall when I heard the pounding of hooves in the distance. My heart leaped.

There—galloping across the snowy field—was Steele. He was coming in fast. I rushed toward him.

But his face was like thunder, and there was mud all down his right side. He'd had a fall. I felt sick.

"Are you hurt?" I demanded, gut churning.

Rex looked exhausted, drenched in sweat, his muzzle covered in foam, and mud splattered over his belly. Steele dismounted, hauled off the saddle, and tied him to the fence.

"I'm fine," he grunted. He wouldn't even look at me. He hated my guts. My heart broke all over again.

He snatched the rake from me and started mucking out Rex's stable with violent, careless movements. I stood behind him, watching, wringing my hands.

"I'll take you to the airport, put you on the plane," he said in a hard tone, over his shoulder.

"B-but…" I stammered.

"Go find out when the next flight is. I'll give you money for it. And go get your stuff together."

I opened my mouth and closed it again, tears springing to my eyes once more.

"I'm sorry," I whimpered to Steele's broad back. But even

his back seemed to hate me.

I couldn't stand the sight of him being so furious with me anymore.

I turned tail, and ran back into the house.

* * *

I'D HOPED I could spend a little more time at the ranch, getting used to the idea that I was leaving. But Steele wanted me gone ASAP. I guessed I couldn't blame him, but that didn't stop it hurting.

With trembling fingers, I went on the Internet and found a flight that left from Vancouver late that afternoon. It meant a night in the airport, but whatever. I wasn't about to hang around where I wasn't wanted. When Steele burst into the house, slamming the door shut behind him, I told him stutteringly about the flight, and he grabbed the laptop and bought me a ticket.

"Can I say goodbye to the animals?" I asked.

"Whatever you want," was his grunted reply.

I stopped by the cowshed and stroked Daisy. I'd come to enjoy the peaceful rhythm of milking her every day.

Then I went to the stalls and said goodbye to the horses. I was sad to see each one for the last time, but when I went to Megan's stall and pressed my face against her soft nose, yet more tears leaked from my eyes. I was going to miss her so badly. Steele had said we were bonding, and he'd mentioned that maybe I could take her to some local shows in the spring. Well, that wasn't going to happen now. This life wasn't mine any more. I was going to have to get used to junk food and cigarette smoke and blaring TV again.

And no Steele.

The thought echoed around my insides like an endlessly ricocheting ball, hollowing me out with each agonizing blow.

I hardly put anything in my backpack. I couldn't stand to take all my beautiful clothes out of the closet—all the things Steele had bought for me with such care. Instead, I grabbed the couple of scrappy things I'd been wearing when I arrived, and a few toiletries.

Steele came into the mudroom when I was still deliberating over whether to bring the cowboy boots with me. "Ready?" he demanded.

There was such coldness and brutality in his eyes, I could have sworn my heart stopped beating. "Guess so," I replied.

Before I knew it—long before I was ready—we were in the truck, and Steele was driving me away from my home for the last time. He wouldn't look at me, and I couldn't stand to see him like this, either. His cold fury was unbearable. But I deserved every drop of it.

The sky was yellowish, and the landscape was blanketed in snow, and it all looked desolate and alien. I had a sense that I was leaving behind every part of myself that mattered, as if I was splitting in two, and the good parts of me were staying at the ranch like a ghost, while my old self was returning to Texas.

THREE HOURS LATER, Steele pulled up in front of the departures sign at the airport.

"Here you go," he said.

I turned my head to look at him, and was stunned by the anguish in his eyes.

"You know I have to do this, Steele," I told him. "But I really don't want to."

"You made your choice, Carrie," he replied brusquely.

"Maybe I can come back one day—" I started to say, then realized that was a shitty thing to say. He was hardly going to welcome me back with open arms when I'd left him like this.

He held out his arms. "Come here."

I fell into him with a gasp, but his embrace was stiff and cold.

And he drew back fast. I choked up again as I turned to open the door and climbed out of the truck.

I couldn't bear to look back, but I heard him drive away before I'd even entered the revolving doors of the airport.

* * *

I'D NEVER BEEN on a plane before, but I was too miserable to be nervous about the unfamiliar process. The border officer asked why I didn't have an entry stamp. I played dumb and said I'd come in on a bus tour and they must have forgotten to stamp it. She scanned my red eyes and trembling mouth, and her eyes turned soft. She told me to be more careful next time.

I trudged to the departure gate, and before I knew it, I was up in the sky, looking down on endless white fields. My eyes were stinging but dry. I felt flat, deadened with loss.

I'd been messaging with Destiny, and she was saying what a dick Enzo was being. Apparently, he was more full of himself than ever since he'd gotten back from hospital, because he really believed he was some kind of hero. I didn't want to ask her if he was being sleazy and risk putting the idea in her head. But I could imagine those piggy eyes of his gawking at her. She was pretty and innocent, and Enzo just loved breaking things. The sooner I got back there, the better —I knew that.

But it didn't make me feel any better about Steele.

I arrived in Denver airport two-and-a-half hours later. Steele had given me a wad of cash, even though I'd tried to refuse it. My wages for five hours' work per day since I'd been at the ranch, he told me. And somehow that hurt as much as anything. He was trying to act like I was an employee who'd come to the end of her employment. Maybe that was how he'd think about me in future. He'd told me to get a hotel at the airport. But I didn't even go look. I didn't want to be comfortable. Instead, I got chicken nuggets, then I lay down on a bench in the quietest spot I could find, and prepared to wait out the hours until my connecting flight took off.

It was a long, miserable night. The lighting was bright, the air-con was freezing, and there were noisy announcements all the time. I tossed and turned on the bench, guilty and sad and missing Steele like crazy. Wishing more than anything that I was back in bed with him.

My first night without him. In all these weeks. I wondered if he was asleep, too. If my empty spot in the bed was an insult to him.

I'd done a terrible thing. We'd made a promise to each other—he was my daddy, and he'd made me his little one, and I'd thrown it away like it was nothing.

Every part of me, every nerve in my body, called out to him. I wished I could take it all back. Things had seemed so simple—just the two of us and the animals, and the ranch our whole world. But all the time, I'd been scared to trust our happiness, to fully let down my guard. I'd always been worried that Enzo would pop up again and ruin things. And now it had happened.

I could deal with Enzo; I'd have to. But in the process, I'd hurt my daddy. Every time I thought of the confusion and anger in Steele's face yesterday, my gut churned and I felt like I was going to be sick.

What we'd had was so special. Once in a lifetime. I'd had one good thing in life—I'd been lucky enough to find the best man, and I'd blown it. Whatever happened, he'd never let me come back now.

CHAPTER 19

Carrie

*J*ust after seven a.m., my phone alarm went. I needed to get up and take myself to my departure gate. I hauled myself up off the bench and stretched my sore muscles. My eyes were gritty, my head was pounding, and my mouth felt like sandpaper. I grabbed my water bottle from my bag and had a swig. As I straightened up again, I saw a tall cowboy was walking toward me from the far end of the building. It was a mirage created by my sleep-deprived brain.

I rubbed my eyes, trying to clear my vision.

The figure was still there—tall, broad-shouldered, and wearing a black cowboy hat—striding purposefully toward me.

It can't be.

Could it?

My broken brain was playing tricks on me. I sat paralyzed, staring stupidly as he approached.

Then my heart began to flutter like a bird taking flight.

"Steele?" I croaked as a familiar, much-loved face came into view. Unmistakable.

He walked faster, swept in, and caught me up in his arms.

"I'm here, babygirl," he said. He lifted me right off the ground. I wrapped my arms and legs around him, clinging to him like a child.

I gave a big shudder, then my whole body relaxed. That feeling of *home* washed through me again.

"When did you... What happened—" I stuttered.

"I'm so sorry," he said into my neck.

"Wh-why?"

"Carrie, I should never have put you in that position—made you feel like you had to choose. I should've respected your relationship with your family."

He released his hold on my legs, and my feet slid down to the ground. I let him guide me to the bench and we sat down together. There were dark shadows under his eyes and tense lines around his mouth. He was exhausted.

I shook my head, confused. "I don't understand—"

"Let me finish, Carrie," he continued, squeezing my hand. "Of course you want to take care of your cousin. It's because you're a good-hearted person, which is one of the things I love most about you. I shouldn't have seen it as a rejection of me. I was just..." He broke off and stared up at the ceiling. "I've been scared of losing you. This whole time. So when this situation came up, it just seemed like confirmation."

I blinked. "But why were you scared? I'm the lucky one to be with you."

He shook his head, a smile playing at his lips. He raised my hand and kissed it. "Carrie, you're a very special person. You have no idea. But I always thought you might run off one day, like a wild pony. You might wake up one morning and realize you don't enjoy our dynamic anymore."

I stared at him in amazement. "Are you kidding? Being with you, as my daddy, makes me the person I was always supposed to be."

He sighed. Then he looked at his watch. "I've been a fool. But I'm going to fix that now. I still don't want you going to Texas, Carrie. It's dangerous. So I'm going to go instead. Deal with Enzo, once and for all."

I gaped. "But how?"

He got that serious look on his face again—his *Daddy* look, as I called it to myself. "I need you not to ask me anything about this. I just need you to trust that I'm going to act in your best interest, and in the best interests of your mom and your cousin. Can you do that?"

"I-I don't know," I stuttered, my thoughts spinning. *Can I go back to the ranch and leave Steele to deal with my family?* "Why don't I come with you?" I said instead.

"Because I'll be better off by myself," he said gently.

"Enzo has guns," I said.

"Where?"

"Usually shoved down the side of his pants."

"Any others? Does he have an ankle holster?"

"Not that I've ever seen. He's a slob. He's too lazy to prepare himself like that."

"Does your mom keep guns in the house?"

"No. She hates them, actually. Guess she's had too many dickweed boyfriends waving them around over the years."

"Okay, good."

"Steele, I'm worried about you doing this." I clutched his arms. I had no idea what he was planning, and I was scared. I knew Steele was way tougher and smarter than any wannabe gangster. But I also knew he wasn't used to guys like Enzo—

loser gangsters who didn't hold their own lives in high regard, never mind anyone else's.

"Carrie, I need you to trust and to not worry about me. I used to be in the military. I know what I'm doing." He pulled something out of his back pocket. "I've got you a ticket back to Vancouver." He thrust it at me. "Go back to the ranch and stay safe, and I'll be back in a few days."

I stared at the ticket blankly. "I don't like this."

"It's the only way. I'll be safe, and no one's going to get hurt. I promise."

I gazed into his eyes—eyes that were full of love and care for me. I did trust him. And this was the only option that didn't involve me playing right into Enzo's hands.

"Okay," I said reluctantly.

He broke into a smile. "You'll go back to the ranch?"

I nodded. "Yes, I will. And this time, I'm not leaving."

"That's the best news." There was a catch in his voice, and he hugged me tight. "I have to go get this flight."

I followed him to the gate, and he gave me one final hug and kissed my forehead, then my lips. "Take a taxi to the ranch. I'll be back before you know it." His mouth dipped to my ear. "Daddy's taking care of things."

Shivers ran through me, and I nodded.

I watched until he disappeared, giddy with the emotions hurtling through me: shock, relief, and worry. It had all happened so fast; my brain was still catching up.

And my flight was boarding right now, from the other end of the airport.

My legs were wobbly, but I started to run.

* * *

THE SNOW WAS heavy on the roads as the taxi brought me back to the ranch. It had only been twenty-four hours since I'd left, but I felt like I was returning to a long-lost friend. And as we turned onto the dirt road that led to the ranch, and Steele's land came into view, my heart gave a ridiculous leap. I was back again. I could stay here with my daddy, and I didn't have to go back to Texas. I rushed up the steps of the decking and retrieved the key from behind the bench, where he'd left it for me. I wished so badly that Steele was here, too. But I had to trust that he was taking care of himself. Doing something to help me.

I rushed inside the house, and the warmth of home enveloped me. Mine and Steele's home. How could I ever have thought that leaving was a good idea?

Steele had texted me to check that I'd arrived safely. Then he sent me another message:

Don't worry about me, baby. I'll be back soon. I want you to focus on taking care of the animals and staying warm indoors. That's all you need to worry about.

I promised I would, but I was scared for him. I didn't know exactly what he was planning, but the fact he was keeping it from me made me worry it was something dangerous.

I was scared he was underestimating Enzo, too. Steele was smart, and he was interpreting Enzo's motivations with logic. The trouble was, Enzo was dumb. He didn't think like intelligent people did. He just went with whatever shit was in his head at any given time.

If he woke up tomorrow morning, mad that I hadn't come running back to him, he could easily decide to take himself to the police station and announce that I'd stabbed him. He was reckless, impulsive.

But Steele had been in the military; he was highly trained. I needed to remember that, and not let my thoughts run away with me.

Stay safe, Daddy, and come back soon, I prayed, again and again.

And then another message came:

And I want you to keep up your training for two hours every day.

I smirked. I had no doubt what he meant by that. And I was kind of amused that he managed to think about it amid everything else that was going on. While I was still thinking that over, there was one more:

I don't want you to touch yourself, though.

I couldn't help smiling. "Dammit, read my mind," I muttered.

I'm going to check you when I get back, and if I suspect you've had any orgasms without my permission, you're going to be in big trouble.

I rolled my eyes. Knowing Steele, he would know. Hell, he'd probably know from looking into my eyes. I didn't know how I was going to make it through the next few days, though.

* * *

LATER IN THE AFTERNOON, after I'd seen to the animals, a truck pulled into the yard. It was Barbara.

"A little bird told me you were home alone," she called, full of sparkle and enthusiasm. "I've got to cook up a batch of food for some potential buyers who are visiting us tomorrow. I was wondering if you wanted to keep me company while I do that?"

"I'd love to," I said. Anything to get me away from the thoughts and worries that were driving me crazy. I was touched that Steele had thought of it, and Barbara had agreed.

. . .

AN EVENING at Barbara and Tom's cozy ranch was just what I needed.

They had a huge kitchen-diner, with a fire in the corner, and a big wooden table.

Barbara told me she didn't need any help with the food, but I insisted on getting stuck in.

"You've really got a flair for cooking, Carrie, you know that?" she told me.

"Oh, it's nothing." I turned away, feeling shy.

"No, you do," she persisted. "No one ever told you that before?"

I shrugged. "Never really tried it before."

She regarded me with interest. "Maybe think about it? Take some lessons?"

"I will," I said slowly, ideas starting to form in my brain.

They had two kids—five-year-old Jennifer and three-year-old Ryan, who hurtled around, full of energy. Barbara was so good with them. Busy as she was, she stopped and gave them attention whenever they appeared with a question or a request, her face shining with love and patience. I'd never seen adults act like that with children before. Memories of my own childhood featured my mom being out of it, or too upset because going some guy had dumped her, or too caught up with her new guy to pay me any attention at all. But the sight of Barbara with her kids made me realize I wanted kids someday. I'd always thought I wouldn't have the skills to be a good mom. But I started to daydream about having Steele's babies. His seed growing inside me. Me swelling with it every day, until I gave birth to a little baby who would look just like him. Was that what Steele wanted, too? I sure hoped so. But even if he didn't want kids, I knew I'd be happy with just the two of us, and the horses.

Tom brought a bunch of pizzas for dinner and we ate them in the den, straight out of the box.

"A rare treat," Barbara told me with a raised eyebrow. "Usually we eat at the table, but since it's out of action today…"

I grinned, deciding not to mention how I'd been raised.

After Tom had bathed the kids, I offered to read them a bedtime story.

Barbara looked so pleased. "Yes, that would be great, hon. Thanks."

I'd never read anyone a bedtime story before, but it was a lot of fun.

"Go on Ryan's bed because he always falls asleep first," Jennifer told me in her sweet little voice.

I lay on his bed, and the kids picked the book they wanted, and snuggled in on either side of me. When Ryan's little eyelids started to close, Jennifer and I eased ourselves out of the bed, and I tucked him in. Then I went to her side of the room and read her a story for older kids. In a few minutes, she was asleep, too. I pulled up her coverlet and switched off the light, leaving the room lit by moon and star ceiling stickers. *I could get used to that*, I thought.

"Any time you need a babysitter, I'm your girl," I told Barbara, back in the kitchen.

"Careful, I'll hold you to that," she said with a mischievous smile. "Steele will end up lonesome in the evenings."

* * *

THE VISIT HAD DONE me a lot of good, and taken my mind off Steele for a while. But once Tom had dropped me off home, and I'd brushed my teeth and turned off all the lights, my fears rushed back.

When I was getting into bed, Steele texted to say goodnight, and I texted him back. I wanted to tell him how lonely I was without him, to pepper my message with emoji. But I didn't think he'd appreciate that. Instead, I told him I loved him, and I couldn't wait to see him again.

Me too, baby, times a million. I promise this is the last time we'll ever be apart,

he replied.

And then he sent me five red hearts. I ran my pinkie over them, grinning in delight. He was loosening up a lot these days.

I tucked the phone under my pillow, and snuggled in, surrounded by his masculine scent. But it was a long time before I fell into an anxious, broken sleep.

CHAPTER 20

Carrie

*W*hen I woke up the next morning, Steele had already sent a text asking how I'd slept. I replied, but he didn't message back again. All morning long, while I mucked out the horses and checked on the cows, I worried about him.

My heart ached, and I fretted non-stop. The only thing that made me feel better was training myself with the plug, knowing I was doing as my daddy told me.

Preparing myself for him.

I lay down on the bed, pulled my jeans and panties down, and slid the plug into my ass. It was a lot harder do it myself. When Steele put it in me, I was always bent over and open to him, my pussy already wet.

I pulled my jeans back up and did some chores in the house with it still inside me. It was a dirty, taboo feeling—

acting like everything was normal when all the time, this little thing was inside me, driving me crazy.

When Steele got back, I was going to tell him to take my ass right away. I was ready for him. I didn't want to wait any longer. I wanted him to claim me everywhere; make me his in every sense of the word.

* * *

HALFWAY THROUGH THE AFTERNOON, I was hanging over the stable door, petting Megan's velvety face and telling her that Steele would be home soon, when I heard a truck pulling into the yard.

It was too soon for Steele to be back.

But in my excitement, I forgot that.

I rushed around the side of the building, and hurtled toward it.

Then I skidded to a stop. It wasn't Steele's truck. It was a gleaming white GMC.

A tall, broad-shouldered man got out. He turned his head, and the breath left my body. He looked just like Steele, but where my daddy was rough and rugged, this man was sleek and polished as a blade. He had slicked back dark brown hair and an achingly handsome, angular face.

Steele's brother.

Uneasiness prickled in my gut. Steele had said his brother was away in the city for the winter.

He looked surprised to see me. "Well, hello there," he said, and his eyes roved over me, from head to foot. I crossed my arms over my chest, wishing I was wearing a bra, and that there wasn't a bare inch of flesh between the bottom of my T-shirt and the waistband of my jeans. "What do we have here?" The way he said it made my spine stiffen.

"I'm not a what, I'm a person. I'm Steele's girl—his partner," I corrected myself quickly.

"His partner?" Steele's brother cocked his head to the side. "He *is* a dark horse, isn't he? He didn't say anything about having a partner."

"We've only been together a few weeks," I said defensively. "I wasn't expecting you."

He nodded, his eyes never leaving mine. I didn't like the cold, calculating way he looked at me. "I told Steele I was in the city, but it turns out there's something I need here, and I thought I'd drive up and surprise that grumpy brother of mine."

I shrugged. I guessed he had a right to be here. "Okay then."

"Pardon me, where are my manners? I'm Max." He thrust out his hand.

"Carrie." Reluctantly, I put my hand in his.

He took it in a firm grip. His hand was smooth, not calloused like Steele's. "Pleasure to meet you," he said. But then his grip tightened and he pulled me closer. He was plenty strong. "Rather young, aren't you?"

"Plenty old enough." I snatched my hand back. "Excuse me." I turned my back on him deliberately, hoping he'd get the hint.

But he followed me, prowling like a panther. His cologne was sharp and fresh. I hated it.

I opened the door and passed through it quickly. "Something I can help you with?" I said as I started to close it.

"The things I need are in here." He caught the door handle and yanked it open again.

I kept hold of the door handle. "I can get it for you."

"I don't think so." His voice was cold. "This is my ranch, too."

That was true. And even though he made me uneasy, he

was Steele's brother. They'd been raised together. Surely there couldn't be too much wrong with him. What would Steele think if I hadn't allowed his own brother into his house?"

I stepped away from the door. "Okay. Come in."

He gave me a sharp, condescending nod, and strode in like he owned the place.

The back of my neck prickled. This was *my* place, as much as Steele's. He'd told me that. I didn't quite believe him, but still, I felt like I had some rights over it.

Without warning, Max turned and continued along the hallway, peered into the bathroom, then walked right into the bedroom and shut the door.

Shit. Should I have stopped him?

"What is it you're looking for?" I called.

The door creaked open and Max sauntered out. "Nothing that concerns you." He gave me a cool smile. He was handsome, but that smile chilled me.

Max headed for the kitchen, and I backed away.

"It's always interesting to see how my brother lives his life out here," he remarked. His tone was casual and bored, but I gritted my teeth. He'd just admitted to snooping.

"You're not going to find anything in here. But if you tell me what it is you're looking for, I'll go get it for you."

"Or I'll just ask Steele when he gets back." Max didn't bother to look at me as he opened a cabinet above the microwave.

"What are you doing?" I hated seeing him so at home in the ranch house.

He pulled down a bottle and showed me the black label. "Whiskey. Want some?"

I wrinkled my nose and shook my head. That bottle must've been in there for a long while. Steele never drank alcohol in the house.

Max poured his drink and sipped it neat, eyes on me. Studying me.

I had to get out of there. "I've got things to do. I'll see you later." I darted out the door. I went to the barn and took my phone out of my back pocket to text Steele to tell him his brother was there.

I felt a little shaky and wound tight. It was nothing Max had done. I just didn't like him. He looked at me like he'd weighed me in the balance and found me wanting.

Then I stopped. Steele would only be worried. And he was under enough pressure already.

I put my phone away. It was almost time to milk the cow anyway.

I stopped by Rex's stall first. He didn't come over—he was still too wild for that—but I knew he was listening. His ears pricked up, turning back and forth like radar as I chatted to him. I said dumb stuff, telling about my day, or whatever thought came into my head, but I got the impression he liked it. I hoped so, anyway.

Then I went to collect the milking stool and pail. But when I came out of the shed, Max was there, his shadow slanting across the hay-covered barn floor.

"What do you need?" I said in a hard voice, belying the fact my heart was hammering beneath my ribcage.

He looked over my head like I was nothing. "When you said Steele was your partner, what did you mean exactly?"

"I mean, we're together. In a relationship," I snapped, and kept walking toward the cow.

I hoped Max would leave me alone, but of course, he followed.

I ignored him. Instead, I patted Daisy and she mooed plaintively, eager for me to relieve the pressure in her udders. I positioned the stool beside her, sat down and leaned my shoulder against her warm hide, then began to milk her long teats.

"A relationship. You and Steele," Max murmured. He fingered his chin. "Far as I know, my brother doesn't do relationships anymore. Thought he wanted to be alone forever. What made him change his mind?"

I didn't reply, but a flush spread across my chest. I wanted to ask about Steele's past, but it would be wrong. That information was private, and if I wanted to know, I should ask Steele.

Besides, I'd bite my tongue out before asking Max anything.

After a few moments of silence, Max added, "I have to admit, you are cute. For a plaything."

"I'm not Steele's plaything," I snapped.

"No?" Max raised a brow. He looked so much like his brother in that moment.

Anger rose in me, but I kept my jaw clamped shut. He was just trying to get a rise out of me. What I wanted to know was *why*.

"You're a child," Max continued, almost like he was talking to himself. "I can't believe he'd touch you. He must've gotten lonely enough. Or he needed to sate his needs. He always had particular needs." Max was watching me closely.

This time, my cheeks burned. "You don't know what you're talking about." I ducked my head, hoping my blush wouldn't give me away.

"Don't you?" Max chuckled, a low sound that was pure cruelty. "Oh, Steele, you always knew how to pick them. I never thought he'd stoop to seducing innocents. His last lover was a stunner. Has he told you about her?"

My boot knocked the pail, and I accidentally squirted milk onto the ground. I slammed the pail back into position.

"I see," Max continued like I'd answered. "That's why I

came back, actually. To tell Steele Victoria is single again. She's been asking about him."

A lightning bolt of alarm went through me. But I bit my tongue.

"Yeah, fate pushed them apart for a while. But now it looks like it's brought them together again. She's the only one he's ever loved, you know. The only one he brought to live out here on the ranch."

The pail was full. I got to my feet and grabbed both it and the stool.

"Let me carry that for you." Max reached for the pail. But I held on. His big fingers tightened and he ordered me quietly, "Let go."

"Don't tell me what to do," I muttered.

"Why not? Don't you like it?" The purr in his voice made me let go of the bucket. I wanted to be away from him. He straightened, setting the bucket aside. "If you're warming Steele's bed, I'd wager you do."

He stalked forward slowly. I backed away, but my boots hit a hay bale and I had to stop. I stared up at Max's big form, feeling helpless. His dark eyes searched my face.

"Aren't you a sweet little thing?" he said. He didn't touch me, but his gaze was warm, his voice, low and intimate. "Not surprised Steele decided to make you his pet. Or should I say *ponygirl*?"

I stiffened. *He knows.* Max knew everything. Steele must have told him, or maybe he found out from Victoria. *Steele must've done everything with Victoria.* The thought made me sick.

"I just peeked into the barn," Max continued. "Some pretty interesting stuff in there. I was thinking you could come and tell me all about it."

"You thought wrong," I snapped, and tried to duck away.

Max's hand clamped on the back of my neck, just like Steele's did sometimes. But with Steele, I kinda liked it.

I turned and kicked Max in the shin. I wasn't as tame as he thought I was.

His grip tightened, and he wrenched me away before my foot could connect. He was too strong. "Easy," he ordered. He marched me forward, into the part of the barn where Steele and I played.

A hot mix of fury and betrayal churned in my guts. This was mine and Steele's private place. Our training sessions were special, and I had assumed Steele had kept them to himself, as had I. Had he been updating his brother on them this whole time? Swapping stories about how he'd turned me into a ponygirl? His little one?

Max switched on the light and let me go with a light shove. He was getting more handsy by the minute, as if he was testing the boundaries, seeing how much he could get away with.

He looked around, and whistled.

Because, there was all our stuff: the Bible, which I didn't even need to carry on my head anymore; the crop; the flogger; the lunge whip; all the straps. And the harness, hanging from a hook on the wall.

Max walked to it and touched the straps. I cringed. It obviously didn't belong to a horse—it was too intricate, the distances between the buckles too small.

"My goodness." A shark-like smile hovered over Max's lips. "What is *this*?"

"It's none of your damn business," I snarled. I wanted to run, but I didn't want to leave Max in here alone. If he tried anything, I had to be here to stop it. I had to protect the ranch, for Steele.

Max tutted. "My brother's business is my business, sweetie. You'll learn that very soon." He sighed. "We own this place together, did you realize? All of our inheritance, locked into this land. Not worth much, unless Steele sells. And he doesn't want to sell." He gave me a sidelong glance. "There's no money for you, sweetheart."

"I'm not here for money."

"No? You're smarter than Victoria then. Took her a while to figure that out." He turned and suddenly his whole focus was back on me. "What is it you want then? Is it possible my brother is so lucky, he found someone as kinky as he is?"

I realized he had my harness in his hands. I froze, torn between wanting to snatch it back, and wanting to run.

"If it's kink you want, you may as well scene with me. I'll give you what you need," Max went on.

What the hell? I felt like I was going to be sick.

"What do you say, little one?" The endearment sounded wrong coming from him. "Shall I show you what you've been missing?" He prowled forward, looming over me. "Steele never was strict enough with his submissives. That's why Victoria left. If she'd been mine, I would've broken her properly."

"You're a monster." I was shaking, but something made me stand my ground. "This is between me and Steele. What we have is ours, and it has nothing to do with you." I worked up my nerve and snatched the harness out of Max's hands, holding it close. "It's time for you to leave."

"So feisty. This is exactly what I mean." Max made his move, tugging me against him. He grabbed a fistful of my hair, yanked my head back, and brought his head down to mine. Instead of kissing me, he nuzzled my jawline.

I turned my head and snapped my teeth. I bit nothing but air, but he let me go.

"What the hell do you think you're doing?" a voice boomed.

I tore my face away from Max. The barn door was wide open and there was Steele, silhouetted in the doorway.

All the air rushed out of me.

Steele strode across the room, and hauled me away from Max. Then he turned with a snap and landed a punch, right in Max's face.

Max staggered backward. He put a hand to his nose. "Hello, brother. Your little toy and I were just getting acquainted."

"You liar!" I yelled. "He grabbed me."

Max winked at me. "She told me she liked it like that."

My mouth fell open. Fucking asshole. What if Steele believed him?

"That's a lie," Steele snarled. And he launched himself at Max again.

This time, Max got a few punches in. Both brothers were tall and strong, with vicious fighting skills. And Max was younger. But Steele was bigger, and fought like an enraged bull. He grabbed his brother and slammed Max's back against the wall. "Tell me why you're really here."

Max grinned through a bloody mouth. There was no sign of the pretty city boy anymore. "Heard you had a pretty young thing around. Wanted to see if you'd share."

Steele made a sound of disgust and slammed his brother against the wall one more time before backing away.

"Steele!" I rushed to him and threw my arms around him.

He held me tight, his big chest heaving. "What did he do to you, little one? Did he touch you anywhere?"

"No. I'm okay. You got here just in time."

Steele cupped my face. "I'm so sorry, Carrie. I never should have left you by yourself."

"It's not your fault," I said. "I was safe here—or I would've been, if it wasn't for your brother."

"He's no brother of mine." The look Steele gave Max

scared me. It was so cold, so full of murderous rage. "I won't forgive you for this," he told Max. "You and I are over, for good."

Max pushed himself up from the floor. For the first time, he looked uncertain. "Forgive me if I overstepped the mark," he began. "I was just having a little fun. I thought she was like Victoria."

"She's not."

"I didn't realize she was so important to you—"

"Didn't realize the woman I live with is important to me?" Steele cut in. "What a bunch of horseshit. You turned up and thought you could fool around with someone you thought wasn't strong enough to fight you off." He turned to me. "Is that about right, Carrie?"

I nodded.

Max straightened his suit jacket. He was more beat up than I'd realized. He had a split lip, a cut across his cheek, the start of a black eye, and his cuff was torn.

And he was laughing. A crazed chuckle escaped his bloodied mouth. "Guess you found one worth fighting for," he said.

"What the hell?" Steele thundered. He was mad enough to cuss.

"I never thought I'd see the day. Not after you moped around for years over Victoria." Max shook his head, still chuckling. "Congratulations," he said to me. "What's your name again?"

I made a sound of disgust. Steele stepped between us. "Get out."

"Seriously?" Max looked like he was going to start laughing again. Mad Max. Ugh. "Thought we were brothers. Thought you and I were all we had."

Steele shook his head. "No. No more chances, Max. I'm done with you. Done with your drinking and trying to poach my women. Done with your demands. You're gonna leave right now, and I'll never see you again. I'll pay you your half of the inheritance, sometime in the next week, right into your account. And that's it. I ever see you on this property again, I'll kill you with my bare hands. I swear it."

Max's nostrils flared—the same as his brother's. He looked from me to Steele. "So it's like that, then," he murmured. A little more blood trickled from the corner of his mouth.

"Yeah. You don't come here and harm my girl," Steele said. "Now, go. Get out of my sight."

With one final nod, Max strode out of the barn.

Steele and I stood, looking at each other in silence, until the door of the truck slammed, the engine started up, and the vehicle moved across the gravel track.

"He's gone," Steele said, then he took me in his arms again. "I'm so sorry, babygirl," he muttered, over and over, his breath warm in my hair.

"You've got nothing to be sorry for," I said. I hooked my fingers into the waistband of his jeans. "Let's go inside."

* * *

STEELE LOOKED LIKE HELL. Under the kitchen lights, I saw he had dark shadows under his eyes, and his face was pale and drawn.

"I'll fix some food for us, then we'll talk about everything," I told him, suddenly feeling like the grown up.

He sat down on the couch, and picked up Max's whiskey glass and examined it disgustedly. "I never thought he'd turn up here."

I took it from him gently and dropped it in the bin. Then I let Steele have some time to himself. I knew what he'd said to his brother was a big deal, and he needed to process it.

I heated up a steak pie and roast potatoes. By the time he took his place at the table, he'd perked up a little, and we dug into our food. Turned out, I was starving. I'd lost my appetite while he was away, and it was back with a vengeance. I was bursting to ask Steele what had happened in Texas, but I knew he'd tell me when he was ready. He didn't like to discuss serious stuff at the table. He preferred to talk when we were physically connected, so he could check in with how I was feeling. Another one of the things I loved about him.

When we were done, I lit the fire and we sat down together. I felt bad that he'd come back to that situation with Max. I rubbed his thigh, wondering if he'd been happy before he'd opened the barn door.

"What's wrong, baby?" he asked.

I sighed. " I feel guilty that you've disowned your brother because of me."

He gave a sigh, too—a drawn out one, full of sorrow and resignation.

"The truth is, I didn't tell you the half of it." He squeezed my hand. "I hoped I wouldn't have to share the tawdry details with you. Max and I have always been more rivals than brothers. He competed with me for Dad's attention. When we both got equal shares of the inheritance, he made it clear he wanted out. He even got Victoria to work on me. She didn't want the ranch, either."

"Did he and Victoria…" I couldn't finish it. I couldn't imagine someone cheating on a man as great as Steele.

"Yeah. That was the last straw that broke my relationship with her." He rubbed his face with a rough hand. "She and I had been unhappy for a long time, though. I think she did it as a way out. Or maybe as a way to wake me up, make me stake my claim and do what it took to make her happy." He took my hand again. "But I didn't want her. And now I know why. Max did me a favor, getting her out of my life."

225

"Maybe that's what he was trying to do again." I couldn't believe I was standing up for Max.

Steele snorted. "Maybe. I just never thought he'd turn up here. I never would've left you alone if I'd have known…"

I took his face in my hands and turned it toward me. "Now, you need to stop feeling guilty," I told him. "You couldn't have predicted this." I dipped my head and kissed him, and his big chest rose and fell.

"I love you so much, little one," he said.

I grinned. "I know you do. That is—unless you're going to get back with Victoria?"

Steele shook his head. "What?"

I swallowed hard. "Max said he met her recently, and learned she was single again. Which is apparently why he was going to see you. He said she was your first and only love."

Steele's nostrils flared, and he exhaled hard. "He said that to test you. Victoria and I were lovers, but we weren't in love. She liked the idea of being mine and living on the ranch. But not the reality. I realize that now."

"Really?"

"I was alone when I was with her, Carrie. And when she left, I built up my walls."

"Steele walls?"

He tweaked my nose. "I always thought it was my lot in life to be alone. Never met a woman I truly clicked with. Until…" He stroked my hair. "Until a little ragamuffin turned up on my doorstep one day. And it turned out she was my soulmate."

My heart lifted right up and I threw my arms around him. We kissed again, deep and long.

When we finally pulled apart, I looked at him seriously. "Now, are you going to tell me where you've been?"

He gave a deep nod, and nerves flickered in my stomach as I wondered what he could be about to say.

But he flashed a smile. "I think you're going to be pleased with this." He picked up his phone from the coffee table and scrolled through his apps until he got to his photo stream. As I watched, burning with curiosity, he located a video and pressed play.

My mom's face filled the screen. She seemed to be sitting in the parking lot of Target, and she looked more bedraggled than I remembered. Maybe she'd looked like that for a long time, and I hadn't noticed. Her hair was frizzy and the roots badly needed retouching, and the smoking wrinkles across her upper lip had gotten deeper. Her eyes were pink from crying, as was the tip of her nose.

"Carrie, honey—" She blinked rapidly. "I'm so sorry I sent that stupid message the other day. Enzo made me do it. But that was wrong. I never should have put him ahead of you. Or any of the guys I've been with throughout your life. You're the most precious thing to me in the world. The only precious thing. Enzo's gone now. He's not coming back. I know I've been a terrible mom and I don't deserve to have you as a daughter. I don't expect you to come back to me. But if you could forgive me some day, that's all I could ever ask of you…" She broke off and started sobbing. The video ended.

"She was real sorry," Steele said. "I didn't scare her. We went out for a walk together and had a chat. She feels very guilty about what she did."

"I know she does," I said. "She doesn't usually apologize for anything."

Steele rubbed my back in comforting circles. "You don't have to rush to forgive her, you know. She's not expecting that from you."

I nodded. "It'll take a while. That's for sure."

"I told her about our life up here, how you were. She said you always loved horses."

"Told you!" I said triumphantly. "You thought I was lying, didn't you?"

A smile tugged at his lips. "I didn't know what to think. She said she was real happy we're together. That I was obviously a good guy. And I reminded her of a young Robert Redford."

I burst out laughing. "Yeah, that sounds like Mom."

"And she gives us her blessing to get married, and hopes we might see it in our hearts to invite her," he continued.

I bit my lip. I didn't even know what to say about that.

"I also took Destiny back to her mom, and we had a long chat. She's just got out of rehab. I told her she needs to take responsibility for her daughter, and not leave her with strange men. She agreed and cried a lot." He shrugged. "Sounds like she meant it."

"I sure hope so," I said. "The main thing is Destiny's not with Enzo. What happened to him?"

Steele's expression turned cold but his voice was gentle. "You don't need to know."

My eyes widened. "Did you kill him?"

"He decided to take a vacation in Mexico. A long one. He might never be back."

I opened my mouth to ask more questions but Steele lifted my hand and kissed it. "It's late, babygirl. And I can't wait to hold you in my arms. Shall we go to bed?"

More questions burned on my lips, but Steele was looking at me so tenderly. And did I really need to know what had happened? All that mattered was that Daddy had taken care of it.

Daddy would always take care of everything.

That night, I got tender Steele. He turned off the lights, and he gently undressed me, tracing his lips over every inch of my body. Saying how much he loved me; how precious I was.

He took his time, driving my desire for him, teasing me until I was ready to scream. When he finally entered me, it felt like home. He and I were the whole world, and nothing else mattered.

Nothing would tear us apart again.

CHAPTER 21

Carrie

$\mathcal{T}$he next morning, I woke up in Steele's arms, surrounded by his smell. *He's back*, I thought, and a grin spread across my face. The two nights we'd been apart felt like a year.

"I'll never leave you again," he'd promised me as we drifted off to sleep last night. "If I ever have to go away again, you're coming with me."

My whole body buzzed with relief and happiness. The shock and stress of the past couple of days was already fading away. For the first time since we'd met—since that day he'd found me curled up on his porch—I didn't need to worry that my past was going to catch up with me. I could just look to the future, with him.

Steele and I were together again, and nothing was going to change that.

As we mucked out the horses, Steele seemed wired, excitable. I wondered what he had in store for me.

"How did your training go while I was away?" he asked, while I was brushing Megan's mane.

I stilled. It *had* occurred to me that he hadn't mentioned it so far. I'd thought he'd forgotten about it amid all the events of the last couple of days. How naïve I was.

"It's been going well," I told him.

He nodded, prompting me to say more.

"I wore it for an hour both days, just like you told me to."

A smile tugged at the corners of his mouth. "And did it turn you on, little one?"

"Maybe," I said, my cheeks warming.

"But did you touch yourself?"

"No. I was a good girl. I knew my daddy would punish me if I did."

He looked at me suspiciously. "And how do I know you're telling the truth?"

A little tremor went through me. "Because I always tell the truth these days—since you trained me."

"Let me see," he demanded. "Go get the plug, and go through to the bedroom."

He led Megan back into her stall, and I went inside.

The plug was already in the drawer of my nightstand. Steele looked pleased.

"Now, take off your jeans and panties, and show me how you inserted it."

Hurriedly, I stripped off, then I lay down my back and spread my legs. Steele watched me with a critical eye.

I rubbed the end of the plug over my pussy, and in seconds, I was wet, turned on by Steele's attention, by the hunger in his eyes.

When the plug was thoroughly coated in my wetness, I began to push it into my little hole.

I heard his breathing getting heavier, and saw that telltale stormy look come into his eyes.

With a little pop, the plug went in, and I let go of it, arousal instantly flooding my body.

"You're very wet," he murmured.

"*Mmm,*" I said.

"Were you wet yesterday, and the day before?"

"Yes." I squirmed on the bed, uncomfortable about lying there spread out like that, but well aware what the punishment would be if I decided to move without his permission.

When he laid his hand flat on my pussy, my whole body jolted.

"You feel like you haven't come for a while," he said casually.

"*Mmm,*" I agreed, pressing my lips together. His touch was driving me crazy, and I was about ready to start humping his hand.

He ran his fingertips over my shaven labia. Then he gave me a few light slaps. I put my hands over my face. I loved it when he played with my pussy like that. It felt kind of shameful, but all the more arousing for that. My insides ached like never before, longing to be filled by his cock.

Instead, he teased my clit maddeningly, circling around it with a light fingertip. I clamped my hand over my mouth to stifle my moans.

"You need to come, don't you, little one?"

"Yes," I managed to say.

"You think you've earned it?"

"Uh huh."

He looked dubious. "I don't know." His fingers kept circling, teasing.

"Please!" I choked out.

He raised an eyebrow. "Please, what?"

"Please let me come, Daddy."

A grin spread across his face. At last, he began to rub my clit back and forth, knowing exactly how to touch me, how to bring me to a climax.

I trembled and gasped, and a minute later, I exploded—shuddering all over, with the plug in my ass, and him watching it all happen.

"Beautiful," he murmured appreciatively. "I hope that was worth waiting for."

"It was," I muttered. But I wasn't done yet. The climax had been strong, but only Steele's cock would quell that deep, burning ache.

I prepared to get on my hands and knees, expecting him to fuck me, but instead he told me to put my clothes on and come outside.

A little dazedly, I got dressed again, leaving the plug where it was.

I followed him out to the yard, very aware of the plug stimulating my ass, giving me that weird open-but-full feeling, keeping my arousal at a tipping point.

"I'm going to lunge Rex," Steele announced, like nothing unusual was happening.

There was nothing for me to do. I just hung over the fence as usual while Steele led the crazy horse out of the stable and into the corral. At first, Rex seemed as wild as ever, bucking and squealing, but little by little, Steele calmed him, and after a while he let Steele throw a blanket over his back and trotted along, snorting and sweating, but as calm as a stallion like Rex could get.

I leaned on the fence post and watched, but most of my attention was given over to Steele's plans for me. My nipples were painfully hard beneath the lace of my bra, and my panties were soaked. The seam of my jeans was rubbing my clit and I knew it wouldn't take much encouragement for me to come again. I only hoped he wouldn't make me wait much longer.

When Steele was finally done bringing the wild stallion under control, he led him to the gates of the corral. As he exited, he paused and turned to me like an afterthought.

"Go to the barn," he told me. "Take everything off, except for the plug, and wait for me on the hay bale. On your knees."

I hurried along, excitement and trepidation tingling in my stomach. When I pushed open the door of the barn, I paused, remembering everything that had happened yesterday. How bad things could have turned out.

And how my daddy had saved me.

I could forget about Max now, I told myself. This barn was ours again. Mine and Steele's. Our special place for pony training.

I strode across the wooden boards in the cowboy boots that Steele had bought me all those weeks ago. Then I sat on the hay bale and stripped them off, followed by my jeans, shirt, bra and panties. I put them aside and took up my usual position—kneeling, thighs wide apart, back straight, hands clasped behind my back, and breasts thrust out.

Then I took a deep, calming breath and waited for my daddy.

I OFTEN MADE out I hated the way he made me wait. But it wasn't true. It was like meditation for me. A way for me to get myself out of our normal life and into a headspace where I obeyed Steele's orders unquestioningly. He'd told me that our life wouldn't be about discipline 24/7. That once I was trained, he wouldn't need to give me orders all day long. That he loved my strong personality and didn't want to crush it. But when we were here, in the barn, I would always be submissive to him, and that was how I liked it.

At long last the barn door banged and I heard Steele enter. I longed to turn my head and watch him approach, but part of this pose was for me to look straight ahead, eyes downcast, just waiting for him.

He walked in front of me.

"You look so beautiful, little one," he told me.

I glanced up curiously. He didn't normally speak to me so softly in the barn. And he nearly always made me wear the pony harness.

Instead, he sat down in front of me and kissed me on the mouth, lightly at first, but then deeper and deeper, his hands running all over me, caressing my breasts, my aching cunt. When he fingered me, a groan escaped my lips.

"What do you want, little one?"

"I want you inside me," I said.

He took hold of the end of the plug and tugged on it. A fresh surge of arousal bloomed inside me.

"You want me here?" he demanded.

"Yes," I answered, and heat flooded my cheeks.

"You want your daddy to take your tiny bottom hole?"

"I want you to take me everywhere," I told him.

His handsome face lit with desire. He stood up and stripped his clothes off. I watched, awed all over again as his big, masculine body was revealed to me. His broad chest, his flat, muscular abs, his big thick thighs and, finally, his huge cock. It was erect, already glistening with pre-cum. He stood at the end of the hay bale, gripping his shaft in his hand. "Come here," he told me.

Knowing what he wanted, I crawled toward him on my hands and knees, already parting my lips, ready for him.

His cock slid into my mouth. These days, I could accommodate him. I'd learned how to take it deep, how not to choke when his cock pushed the back of my throat. He held my head and thrust in and out, just the way I liked it. So hot, so dirty, to be used like that.

"Good girl," he murmured. "You suck Daddy's cock so good."

The ache in my pussy got stronger, and it started to clench in little spasms. He withdrew from my mouth and walked behind me, holding his cock casually in his hand like a tool.

He entered me in one quick thrust, and I cried out. The sensation was different from before—more heat, more friction. He wasn't wearing a condom, I realized. He thrust slowly, three, four, five strokes, and I exploded. A sharp, bright orgasm, rippling around his bare girth.

Then he slid out of me, and slowly, slowly pulled the plug out of my ass.

I heard something being squeezed from a bottle. "Some lube," he said. Then I heard a tacky sound as he spread it over his cock. Preparing it for me.

I trembled on my hands and knees, ready for him, aching for him to finally take my ass.

When the head of his cock pressed against my hole, it felt like a release. Waves of pleasure radiated out all over me. He eased himself inside and my muscles relaxed, accommodating him, until it got to the widest bit, and it was hard to take. But he went slow, easing back then pushing forward, little by little, until suddenly, there was a little flowering of pain, and my asshole was gripping his shaft.

I gasped—in shock, discomfort, joy, all rolled into one. Steele was finally taking my ass. My most private place was wide open to him, filled with his cock. My pussy throbbed intensely.

Slowly, he slipped in all the way, and it didn't hurt. A slight, uncomfortable, awkward feeling gave way to pleasure; to the pure bliss of having him possess me everywhere.

"Oh baby, you feel so good," he muttered, his voice tight with the effort of moving slow in my ass. So different from my pussy. More dirty, more shameful.

But so right.

I gripped him tight while his cock slipped in and out, his balls pressing against my pussy.

He pulled me up into his arms, one hand caressing my breasts and the other stroking my clit while his big cock fucked my ass again and again and again.

Strong ripples began to build inside me again.

"I'm going to come!" I cried out, partly in surprise. Three more fast strokes, and an intense orgasm ripped through me, my ass spasming around his cock.

"Oh, baby," he gasped in my ear. He started to move harder and faster, and a second later, he came deep inside me, filling my ass with his hot seed.

It was the first time he'd come inside me. So wrong, yet so right that the first time was in my ass.

I gave a sigh of pure pleasure.

Steele came out of me real slow, then he took me in his arms.

"You're fully mine now, little one," he said.

I closed my eyes and leaned my head against his big chest. "All yours," I agreed.

"Forever."

As if sensing I was too overwhelmed to walk, he lifted me up and carried me back inside. Into our house.

Where I was going to live, always—safe and protected by my daddy.

* * *

Steele

THAT NIGHT, when Carrie and I went to bed, I looked at her, sleeping—my little angel. Curled up on her side, her blonde hair neatly brushed, hands tucked under her chin. At last, she looked completely peaceful.

She's mine, I thought and finally, I fully believed it. There was nothing hanging over our heads anymore. No black clouds on the horizon.

As hard as the last few days had been, I was glad things were finally resolved.

And I was full of gratitude that she'd forgiven me for getting so mad at her. All the tensions with our families were finally behind us, and we could relax and look forward to a beautiful future together.

Things wouldn't always be easy—that was how life was. I was going to apply for a mortgage on Monday, and give Max his money. His out. I didn't need him anymore. Carrie and I could decide what to do about the guest houses and the tourist side of the business. She could play hostess as long as she wanted, or we could close it up.

And I expected that I would need to keep tabs on Enzo for a long time—not because I was worried he'd try to hurt Carrie, but because I cared about Carrie's mom. She'd been a useless parent, but she'd had a hard life, too. It was a chain of neglect, most likely stretching back for generations.

But it ended here—with me and Carrie. I swore she would never experience a moment of fear and abuse in her life again. I would protect her with my last breath. Make sure every day was full of all the happiness she deserved.

My little one and I would never be parted again.

***

Want more Steele & Carrie? Click here to read an exclusive extra Steele Breeds His Babygirl. Go here to download: https://geni.us/Steeleandbabygirl

Next is Joel's book...find it here.

Bad Boy Alphas with Renee Rose (bad boy werewolves)

Never ever date a werewolf.

Tsenturion Masters with Golden Angel

Who knew my e-reader was a portal to another galaxy? Now I'm stuck with a fierce alien commander who wants to claim me as his own.

ABOUT LEE SAVINO

Lee Savino has plans to take over the world, but most days can't find her keys or her phone, so she just stays home and writes smexy (smart + sexy) romance. She loves chocolate, lives in yoga pants, and looks great in hats.

For tons of crazy fun, join her Goddess Group on Facebook or visit www.leesavino.com to sign up for her mailing list and get a free book.

Website: www.leesavino.com

ABOUT TRISTAN RIVERS

Tristan Rivers has been writing romance full-time for the past five years—which is the best job in the world, of course :D

She has a thing for hands— big, rough hands that can turn gentle enough to leave you breathless. She also loves work-toughened leather and wild open spaces.

Her heroes are bossy but kind, and her heroines are most definitely in need of a firm hand!

She lives in Colorado with her husband and two mischievous rescue mutts.

Be sure to download the extra freebie with Carrie & Steele so you can follow her new releases! Go here to download: https://geni.us/Steeleandbabygirl